A Heart Full of Hope

An Addy Classic
Volume 2

by Connie Porter

★ American Girl®

Published by American Girl Publishing
Copyright © 1994, 1998, 2000, 2014 American Girl

Questions or comments? Call 1-800-845-0005,
visit **americangirl.com**, or write to Customer Service,
American Girl, 8400 Fairway Place, Middleton, WI 53562.

Printed in China
14 15 16 17 18 19 20 LEO 10 9 8 7 6 5 4 3 2 1

This book is a work of fiction. Any similarity to real persons, living or dead,
is coincidental and not intended by American Girl. References to real events,
people, or places are used fictitiously. Other names, characters, places, and
incidents are the products of imagination.

Cover image by Michael Dwornik and Juliana Kolesova

Cataloging-in-Publication Data available from the Library of Congress

*For my parents
and my nieces and nephews*

*To my editor, Bobbie Johnson—
thanks for helping bring Addy to life*

Beforever

Beforever is about making connections.
It's about exploring the past, finding your
place in the present, and thinking about the
possibilities your future can bring. And it's about
seeing the common thread that ties girls from
all times together. The inspiring characters you
will meet stand up for what they care about
most: Helping others. Protecting the earth.
Overcoming injustice. Through their courageous
stories, discover how staying true to your own
beliefs will help make your world better
today—and tomorrow.

TABLE *of* CONTENTS

Double Dutch

he jump ropes slapped on the sidewalk as
Addy took her place at the end of the line
of girls who were playing Double Dutch
after school. Addy had just missed for the fourth time.

"Don't worry," said her good friend Sarah. "Just
keep trying. You'll get it. Double Dutch is hard."

Addy agreed. "It sure is. I can jump with one
rope just fine. But the minute I try to jump into two,
I get all tangled up. The ropes go so fast, I can hardly
see them."

"That'll change," said Sarah. "Just don't get discouraged."

In spite of her troubles with Double Dutch, Addy
felt happy on this pretty spring day. Poppa had been
back with her and Momma for three months. They had
moved out of Mrs. Ford's garret and into a boarding

house. It was almost like having a big family again, except that Addy's brother Sam and baby sister Esther weren't there. *Maybe that'll change someday, too,* she thought.

"Look it there," Sarah said, pointing up the street. "Ain't that your poppa driving the ice wagon?"

Addy looked where Sarah was pointing.

"That's Poppa!" Addy exclaimed. "Let's go meet him." The girls took off and raced down the block.

"Well, well," Poppa said in his deep voice when the girls reached the wagon. "Look what the wind done blown my way. I reckon you girls could use a nice chunk of ice to cool you down."

"I sure could," said Sarah, panting from the run.

"Me, too," said Addy with a smile.

Poppa got down from his seat. The girls followed him to the back where he opened the doors of the wagon. Inside were huge blocks of ice. Addy could feel a moist coolness come from inside. Poppa slipped on a pair of thick gloves and took an ice pick from his belt. As he chipped away at a block of ice, glittering slivers flew into the air. He handed Sarah and Addy each a piece of ice the size of a small slice of pie.

"If you girls want a ride home, I'm gonna be heading that way in a bit. I got a few stops to make first,"
Poppa said.

"We'd like to ride. Come on, Sarah," Addy said.

"I can't," said Sarah. "I got to get right straight
home and help my momma."

"All right," Addy said. "I'll see you tomorrow." She
was disappointed. Sarah often had to help her mother
do the washing that she took in to earn money.

Addy and Poppa climbed onto the wagon as Sarah
left. Poppa slapped the reins on the horse's back, and
the wagon moved away from the curb.

Addy sat close to Poppa, sucking on her piece of ice.
It was like holding a piece of winter. Addy had to shift
it from hand to hand as it slowly melted and dripped.
Poppa gave her his huge gloves.

"Wear these," he said, "so your hands won't get
cold."

"I wish Sarah ain't have to help her momma so
much," Addy said as she put the gloves on.

"I wish she didn't neither," Poppa said, "but her
family need the money." He shook his head. "I never
did expect things to be easy in freedom, but I didn't

think things would be so hard either."

Addy looked at Poppa. His big smile had melted away. His face looked serious.

"When me and Momma first got here, I didn't like Philadelphia at all," Addy said softly. "Momma worked real hard, and I spent most of my time alone in our room. I was missing you and Sam and Esther something awful. But Momma kept saying things was gonna get better. It was gonna take time for things to change."

"Sometimes it seem like change is as slow as this here tired old horse," Poppa sighed. "But at least in Philadelphia, things can change for the better."

"That's true," Addy said, finishing her ice and removing Poppa's gloves. "When we was down on the plantation, there was no chance for things to change."

"Slavery was draining the life out of all of us," said Poppa. "That's one reason I knew we had to take our freedom."

Addy spread out her arms. "Here in Philadelphia, it seem like my world getting bigger and bigger. Sometimes I can't believe I really go to school, that I can read and write and do my figures. I used to dream about it, but now it's real. And look at us, Poppa. We riding around the city on this big wagon! This is much better than worming tobacco plants."

Addy saw a smile ease back onto Poppa's face.

Poppa said, "There *is* some things better here. You going to school, me and your momma getting *paid* for our work, and we got a nice room at the boarding house."

"Even though Sam and Esther ain't with us yet," Addy said, "you being here done made things much better for me and Momma."

"But I want them to be even better," Poppa responded. "Hauling ice don't take nothing but muscle. I'm a good carpenter. I got a good mind. I can build anything. Every carpenter job I try to get, they say they don't hire colored folks. Ain't that something, Addy? When we was in slavery, I was a carpenter. Now that I'm free, I find out these white people up North think a colored man ain't good enough or smart enough to drive a nail."

"That ain't fair," Addy said.

"Sure ain't," Poppa said. "But that's the way it is."

Poppa made two deliveries before he came to his

last stop at Natkin's Confectionery Shop. Addy could see a group of white girls about her age sitting at a table eating ice cream. She had walked by this shop once with Sarah, and Sarah had told her they sold ice cream there. Back then, Addy had not even known what ice cream was, but at a church social a few weeks later, Addy had her first taste of it. She loved it! It was creamy and sweet and cold. Without thinking, Addy blurted out to Poppa, "It sure would be good to have some ice cream now."

As soon as the words had flown out of her mouth, Addy felt awful. She shouldn't ask Poppa to spend money on fancy treats, and she also knew that this shop didn't serve black people. She looked again at the group of girls talking happily inside. Poppa glanced where Addy was looking. He didn't say anything as he climbed down from the wagon.

Addy watched Poppa lift a huge block of ice with a pair of large tongs. He rested it on his shoulder, headed down the alley, and went in the side door of the confectionery. On his way out, Poppa stopped to talk to a white man who gave Poppa a friendly pat on the shoulder.

"Was that Mr. Natkin?" asked Addy.

Poppa climbed back onto the wagon. "Yes," said Poppa. "I'm telling you, Addy, this is some kinda freedom. I can deliver ice to make ice cream, but I can't even buy my own daughter a dish of it."

"That's all right," Addy said. "I don't like it, anyway."

Poppa looked at her out of the corner of his eye. Addy could tell he didn't believe her. "Let me make sure that door is closed," he said, jumping from the wagon.

When Poppa returned, he was carrying something. "Look here at what was in the trash," he said. "It's a busted-up ice cream freezer. I bet I can fix it up. Then we'll make our own ice cream." Poppa gave Addy a playful nudge. "Won't that be nice?" he asked.

"It would be," Addy said.

Poppa tugged on the reins, and the wagon gave a slow lurch forward.

Addy and Poppa rode on in silence. She was thinking, *Momma, Poppa, and I and all the colored people got a strange kind of freedom here in Philadelphia. There are jobs we can't get and shops we can't eat at just because of the color of our skin. It ain't fair.* When Addy thought of it, she felt just as dizzy as she had standing before the spinning loops of the Double Dutch ropes. Being a black girl in Philadelphia was like being outside the loops of those ropes. Inside was a world Addy wanted to enter. But right now, she was standing on the outside looking in. How would she be able to jump into that other world?

Sunshine

CHAPTER 2

hen Addy came home from school the next
day, a small wagon loaded with furniture
was in front of the tall boarding house.
Boarders often moved in and out. Mr. and Mrs. Golden,
who owned the boarding house, rented out five rooms,
but Addy was the only child in the house. She looked
carefully at the things in the wagon, hoping to see
something belonging to a child, maybe a doll sticking
out of a crate. But all she saw was furniture.

Mr. Golden came out of the front door. Addy
thought that his name was perfect for him. His skin
was golden brown. "Good afternoon to you, Addy.
How are you today?"

"Good afternoon, Mr. Golden," Addy said. "I'm
doing fine. Who's moving in?"

Mr. Golden sat down on the front step and wiped

his neck with a handkerchief. "By the looks of all this furniture, you'd think a family of ten was moving in, but it's just one person—my mother."

"Oh," Addy said, a little disappointed that she wouldn't be getting a playmate. "Would you like some help?"

"No, but thank you kindly," Mr. Golden said, getting up from the step. He went over to the wagon.

Addy went up to her family's room on the second floor. She flopped onto her bed and reached for her doll, Ida Bean, who had been lying on her pillow. Addy loved Ida Bean. She could cuddle with Ida and tell her secrets. But even with Ida to keep her company, Addy still felt lonely during the long afternoons. All the adults in the boarding house were at work. Mrs. Golden was busy making supper for everyone and didn't want to be disturbed. Momma and Poppa didn't get home until late. Sometimes they didn't get home in time for the dinner Mrs. Golden served. On those days, Addy still joined the other boarders for supper in the dining room.

This evening was one of those times, so when Mrs. Golden rang her bell, Addy went down to the dining room by herself. She took her place at one of the two tables. Four other boarders sat at that table, but they didn't pay attention to Addy. They were talking about the trouble black people were facing on the streetcars.

"Did you see today's paper?" Mrs. Golden asked. "There was almost a riot on a streetcar downtown. Three colored people were hurt."

"I'm getting too scared to even ride the streetcars at all," one woman said.

A man at the table joined in. "Well, I heard a conductor threw a colored man off the Pine Street streetcar and broke his leg."

"If they'd just let us sit inside, there wouldn't be all this trouble," another young woman at the table added.

"That'll be the day," said Mr. Golden sourly. "I'll be an old man before I see that change come."

Their talk scared Addy. The longer she listened, the less she was interested in her supper. She began playing with the napkin ring, and she only picked at her dinner of oxtail stew and mashed carrots.

After dinner, Addy headed back to her room. She was halfway up the stairs when she heard a bird singing. Quietly, Addy tiptoed back down the stairs. The bird's beautiful song was like a trail that Addy followed down the narrow hall. The trail stopped at the open door of a room at the end. The room was unlit. The faint light from the hall was the only brightness in it.

At first, Addy saw only her own shadow in the room. But as her eyes got used to the dimness, she saw a cage hanging before the window. In it was a small, yellow bird, sitting on a perch singing out happily. She stood at the door for a minute, enjoying its song.

Suddenly a woman's voice interrupted, "You can come in, child."

Addy was so startled, she jumped. She hadn't seen anyone in the darkened room. She moved a few steps inside. The woman lit a kerosene lamp, and Addy saw the furniture she had seen on the wagon earlier in the day. The woman sat in a high-backed rocker next to the cage.

"Good evening, ma'am," Addy said. "I'm Addy Walker. Me and my momma and poppa live upstairs. You Mr. Golden's momma?"

"That's right," the woman answered. "Come on in and meet my bird, Sunny."

Addy went over closer to the cage. It was then that

she saw the woman's eyes. The colored parts of her eyes, the irises, were covered with a cloudy whiteness. Addy stood staring at the woman.

"Didn't know I was blind, did you?" Mrs. Golden asked.

Addy answered quickly, "No, ma'am. If you blind, how did you know I was standing outside your door?"

"I got plenty of ways of seeing," Mrs. Golden answered. "I heard your footsteps. They were soft as a whisper, and they were spaced close together, so I could tell you were a child. How old are you, Addy?" Mrs. Golden asked. "When is your birthday?"

"I'm nine," Addy said. "But I ain't really sure about when my birthday is. I was born in the spring. My momma know that much." Addy felt ashamed that she didn't know her birthday. Her seatmate at school, Harriet, knew when her birthday was. On that day, Harriet's mother had sent fancy raisin tarts for the whole class.

"That's a shame you don't know your birthday," Mrs. Golden said. "Just listening to you talk, I think you were born into slavery."

"Yes, ma'am," Addy said. "How did you know?"

"Well, most slaves don't know their birthday," Mrs. Golden replied. "I was born right here in Philadelphia, but my parents were born into slavery over one hundred years ago. I'm an old woman, you know. I was there the day God invented dirt."

Addy looked at Mrs. Golden in disbelief.

Mrs. Golden laughed so light and high, it made the room seem brighter. Addy joined in with her laughter.

"You real funny, ma'am," Addy said. "My brother Sam would like you. He like riddles and jokes."

"Your brother?" Mrs. Golden said. "You didn't mention him. Does he live here, too?"

"No, ma'am," Addy explained sadly. "We don't know where Sam is. He might still be a slave, but he wanted to be a soldier. He and my poppa were sold off the plantation. Then my momma and me ran away up here. We had to leave my baby sister Esther on the plantation when we left. But someday, we gonna all be together again."

"Slavery has taken a lot away from colored people," Mrs. Golden said. "If we want to get some of it back, we're going to have to take it. It's going to be some time before your family gets back together. But I know one thing you can take for yourself right now, Addy. When-ever you want, you can choose a special day and claim it for your birthday."

Addy had never thought about this before. "That's a good idea!" she exclaimed. "I want me a really special day. I want me a perfect day for my birthday."

"Now, I've told you I've been around a long time, and I never saw such a thing as a perfect day," said Mrs. Golden.

"How about the day that God invented dirt?" Addy joked.

"Oh, no, no," Mrs. Golden said. "Even that wasn't perfect. But there *is* something special in every day."

"How will I know what day is right for my birth-day?" asked Addy.

"You'll just know," answered Mrs. Golden. "When that almost-perfect day comes along, it'll be meant just for you. Now, the day God invented birds was extra special, close to perfect, and I was there for that, too."

Sunny seemed to understand what Mrs. Golden was saying. He sang happily with his head cocked back and his breast puffed out.

"Mrs. Golden, why your bird in that cage? It seem

like he would be sad and lonesome in there all by himself," Addy said.

Mrs. Golden closed her eyes for a moment before she answered. "I can tell you're a smart girl. You think about things. I do think Sunny is lonely sometimes. I think I can hear it in his song. But we keep each other company. When I hear him singing out from his soul, it brings sunshine into my life."

Addy thought about that. "But he still locked up."

"Oh, child," answered Mrs. Golden. "That cage can't contain Sunny's spirit. It soars right out from behind those bars. That's what's important for all of us. To let our souls sing out."

"Sometimes it's hard to do that, you know," Addy replied, "to let yourself sing out if you feeling lonely or sad."

"Sure is," Mrs. Golden said, looking right at her. "I'll tell you, Addy. When you first spoke to me tonight, I could hear a touch of loneliness in your voice. But even then, I could hear you singing out."

Addy looked away from Mrs. Golden. Addy knew she was blind, but she felt like Mrs. Golden was looking deep inside her.

"Well, I better be going," Addy said. "I still have lessons to do, Mrs. Golden."

"Don't be a stranger at my door, now," Mrs. Golden said. "Come visit me and Sunny whenever you'd like. And one more thing. Please call me M'dear. That's what my family calls me."

"I will," replied Addy. "I will."

Bitter Medicine

CHAPTER 3

uring the next week, Addy stopped by M'dear's room each day when she came home from school.

"Good afternoon," M'dear would call to her before she even reached M'dear's door. Addy usually did her lessons in M'dear's room, and sometimes M'dear had a treat of benne candy for her when she finished. Addy savored the crispy, sugary wafers filled with sesame seeds while she listened to stories M'dear told her. M'dear told Addy that her father had been a soldier in the Revolutionary War, and that when she had been a chore girl working on Society Hill, Thomas Jefferson had visited a house where she worked. Addy loved the stories M'dear told and was happy that M'dear was her friend.

Addy still spent Saturdays by herself because Poppa

and Momma had to work. But this Saturday was going to be different. Momma had told Addy on Thursday, "I know you enjoy M'dear's company, but she's an old woman. She need her rest. Why don't you ask Sarah to come over on Saturday morning?"

"Do you really mean it, Momma?" Addy had asked. Momma had never let Sarah come over to play before.

"Me and Poppa think you should play together more than you do," Momma said.

Poppa was sitting on the floor piecing together the ice cream freezer he had found. "Maybe Sarah can help you pick a day for your birthday," he said. "Remember, when you pick it, Addy, I'm gonna make you ice cream. And you better hurry. I just about got this old freezer fixed."

When Saturday morning came, Addy couldn't wait for Sarah to arrive. The night before, Momma had saved sweet cornbread for Addy and Sarah to share. Momma said they could have that and some milk for a treat. Addy spread an old blanket on the floor. She placed two small plates, spoons, cups, and the cornbread on it. Then Addy eagerly watched out the window for Sarah.

When she saw Sarah coming up the street, Addy thundered down the stairs to meet her.

Sarah was carrying a bag, and she had a smile on her face.

"What you got in the sack?" Addy asked Sarah.

"It's a surprise," Sarah said as Addy led her inside and up the stairs. When they got to the room, Sarah looked at the spread on the floor. "This real nice, Addy," Sarah said. "It's like having a picnic inside."

"I thought you'd like it," Addy said as she poured the milk into their cups. "You're never gonna guess what Momma and Poppa said. You can help me pick a special day for my birthday."

"I think you should pick it all by yourself," said Sarah.

"I guess you right," Addy responded, taking a sip of milk. "I just can't think of a day I want. Don't none seem right enough."

After they had finished, Sarah held up her sack in front of Addy and said, "Keep your eyes closed and reach inside the sack for a surprise."

"Oh, Sarah!" Addy cried as she pulled out a coil of rope.

"I thought we could practice some Double Dutch," said Sarah. "My momma have so many clotheslines from her washing that my poppa cut me this extra piece for us to jump with."

The girls rushed outside, where Sarah wound the middle of the rope around a lamppost. She held the two ends in her hands and began twirling.

Addy felt a little dizzy as she watched the two loops of the rope cross over one another. Again and again she tried to jump in, but Addy's feet always got tangled in the ropes as soon as she did. Sarah continued to encourage her. "That was a good try, Addy."

Addy was feeling discouraged when she heard M'dear say, "Addy, take your time. Watch the ropes, but listen, too."

Addy looked up to see M'dear sitting at the window. Addy introduced Sarah to M'dear, who asked Sarah to start the ropes again.

"Now listen to those ropes," M'dear coached Addy. "They're singing out a rhythm. Hear it, Addy? 'Tip-tap-tip-tap, tip-tap-tip-tap.' Jump to that rhythm. You can do it."

Addy had never listened to the ropes before. She

had only watched them. Now she rocked back and forth before the twirling ropes, listening, getting her body set to their rhythm. Then she jumped in. She jumped four times before she missed. She had never done so well!

"You getting it," Sarah said. "That was much better."

Addy was encouraged. "Did you see me, M'dear?"

"I saw," M'dear said. "I saw."

Sarah started twirling the ropes again. Addy's hands were sweating with anticipation. *I can do it. I can do it*, she repeated to herself. Addy watched the ropes and listened. Tip-tap-tip-tap. Tip-tap-tip-tap. When she was ready, she leapt in between the loops. She was jumping! Eight times in a row. Ten. Twelve. She was losing count. A big smile burst onto Addy's face. Sarah shrieked with delight. Then the ropes twisted around Addy's feet.

Sarah rushed to Addy and gave her a hug. "I knew you could do it, Addy. You was great!"

"I can't believe it," Addy said happily. "I finally got it." She turned to the window, but M'dear was gone.

Addy jumped rope for a while longer. Then Sarah had her turn. When they got tired, they went inside to M'dear's room.

M'dear's door was open, but she was not sitting in her usual place by the window. Instead, she was lying down with a wet cloth on her forehead. Sunny was silent.

"M'dear, you feel all right?" Addy asked softly.

"I was just resting," answered M'dear. "I have a terrible headache, and I've run out of medicine."

"I'll go to the druggist and get you some more," Addy offered. "It's only a few blocks from here. Sarah will go with me."

"If you're sure it wouldn't be any trouble," said M'dear.

"We'd be glad to go," Addy assured her, taking the blue bottle from the table next to M'dear's bed. "We'll be back real quick."

M'dear gave Addy fifty cents. "Get yourselves a treat while you're out getting my medicine," M'dear said. "And bring back the change."

Addy and Sarah went straight to the drug store, but the clerk said he was out of the medicine M'dear needed. The girls left the shop.

"Now what do we do?" asked Sarah in a worried voice.

"I know where there's another drug store on Pebble Avenue," Addy said. "I saw it when I was on the ice wagon with Poppa the other day."

"But Pebble Avenue is miles from here," said Sarah.

"We can take a streetcar," said Addy. "We'll be there in no time."

"I don't think that's such a good idea," Sarah said. "You know we can't ride most streetcars."

"But we *got* to get M'dear's medicine," Addy insisted. "I know which streetcars colored people can ride."

Sarah thought for a minute. "But they dangerous," she protested.

"Not if we stick together," said Addy. "Come on."

Addy and Sarah walked one block to the avenue. They waited only a few minutes before a streetcar came, pulled by two horses. Like the other black riders, Addy and Sarah had to ride on the outside platform. Only whites could ride inside and sit in the seats.

As the horses took off, Addy and Sarah held tightly to the railing. From the first day Addy had arrived in Philadelphia, she had wanted to ride a streetcar. Now here she was! The horses built up speed, and Addy felt a warm breeze sweeping past her. The city whizzed by—the row houses, the markets, the churches. They were a blur kissed by the green of budding trees. As the streetcar slowed, the city came back into focus. When the streetcar stopped for more passengers, the white people paid their fares first. They moved inside, where there were plenty of seats. The black people who came aboard had to squeeze their way onto the outside platform, which was getting crowded. Addy looked at Sarah, who looked worried.

"We almost there," Addy assured her.

The car pulled away so suddenly, the man next to Addy lost his balance and stepped on her foot. The people on the platform were crowded so tightly together now that Addy couldn't feel the breeze as the streetcar gained speed. Addy was relieved when they arrived at their stop and could get off.

The drug store was just a block away from the streetcar stop. The girls took off in a hurry, anxious to get the medicine and return to M'dear. When they reached the store, they found a long line of people waiting at the counter. Addy and Sarah went to the end of the line.

"We'll be on our way in a few minutes," Addy said to Sarah.

The girls inched their way forward in the line. Ten minutes passed before they were up to the counter. Before Addy could open her mouth to ask for the medicine, a man approached the counter. The clerk ignored Addy and waited on him.

"We was next," Sarah whispered to Addy.

"I know," Addy said softly. "Maybe he used to waiting on grown folks first. He probably ain't see us. He gonna wait on us next."

When the clerk finished with the man, Addy started to say, "We'd like to get . . . " Before she could finish her sentence, the clerk walked away to wait on a white girl who had just walked in the door.

"You can't say he didn't see us this time," Sarah said.

Addy knew that Sarah was right. They watched in surprise as the clerk waited on the girl, who was no older than they were. He talked nicely to her as he filled her order. After the girl handed him her money, the clerk gave her back the change, counting it out in her hand.

Finally the clerk came over to Addy. "What do *you*

want?" he asked in a stern voice that startled her.

Addy handed him the medicine bottle and asked for another just like it.

"Do you have money?" he asked.

Addy thought that was a strange question. *Why would I be here if I ain't have money?* she thought. She tried to hand the clerk her money.

"Put it on the counter," he demanded.

Addy glanced at Sarah, who was looking at the floor. As Addy placed the money on the counter, she felt her face getting hot. She was angry and hurt. This was how her master had talked to her on the plantation.

After Addy put the money on the counter, the clerk took it and got the medicine. Then, instead of handing Addy her change, he slapped it down on the counter. Some of it rolled onto the floor. Sarah scrambled to get it. Without saying a word, Addy picked up the medicine and the girls left the shop.

Addy and Sarah started down the avenue, walking hand in hand, to wait for a streetcar to take them back across town.

"That man treated us so bad," Addy said.

"Because we colored," Sarah added. "Some white folks think they're better than us."

"But that's not right," protested Addy, hurt and confused.

"No, it ain't," agreed Sarah. "But things ain't always right."

When they got back to the streetcar stop, a large crowd was waiting impatiently. The first streetcar that came along was packed. It didn't even stop, and some of the people waiting on the corner began to grumble.

"We *gotta* get on this next one," Addy said anxiously. "M'dear waiting for her medicine."

It was twenty minutes before another car came. It stopped and Addy, Sarah, and the rest of the black passengers got on, crowding the platform. As the streetcar pulled out, they were packed so closely that Addy didn't have to hold onto the railing. She held tightly to the bottle of medicine.

At the next stop, the conductor yelled out, "White passengers only!"

A white man made his way through the crowd and got on. He pushed through the black passengers on the platform and sat down in one of the empty seats inside.

"That's not fair," a black man in overalls called up from the street. "We've been waiting for a car for an hour."

A woman standing near the man added, "There's plenty of room if you let us ride inside."

"I don't make the rules," the conductor replied. "You'll have to wait for the next car."

"We won't wait!" the black man in the overalls yelled. He and some of the other people who had been waiting pushed their way onto the car.

The conductor's voice boomed, "Get off of this car! Get off!"

Addy felt her heart beating fast. She looked for Sarah, but Sarah had been pushed past her. As Addy turned, she saw the conductor pushing through the passengers toward the people who had just gotten on the streetcar. Some of them jumped off, but the man in the overalls didn't. He held onto the railing. When the conductor reached him, he grabbed the man by the straps of his overalls and pulled at him until the man lost his grip and fell to the street.

Then the conductor turned to the black people on the platform. "Now, all of you colored people, out!"

he bellowed. His face was red with fury. "Every last one of you!"

"We already paid our fare," one woman protested.

"I don't care," he screamed. "I'll call the police if every last one of you doesn't get off right now!"

Addy felt pushing from all sides. A sharp elbow hit her shoulder. Someone trampled over her feet. Addy was caught up in the crowd, and before she knew it, she was swept right off the platform. She fell to the ground, ripping a hole in her stocking and scraping her knee. She watched the streetcar pull away from the stop with no one on the platform and plenty of empty seats inside.

Sarah rushed up to her. "Addy, is you all right?"

"I guess so," Addy said. "At least I didn't drop M'dear's medicine."

"I don't want to get back on no streetcar," said Sarah.

"Don't worry about that," said Addy. "There ain't no more money for the fare anyway. We used up everything M'dear gave us on the two rides we already took."

"How far is it to home?" Sarah asked.

"It's a long way from here," Addy said. "A long way."

Brotherly
Love

 t was late afternoon when Addy and
Sarah finally made it back to the boarding house. As they trudged down the
hall, M'dear called out, "Addy, is that you and your
friend?"

"It's us," Addy answered. She tried not to sound
as discouraged as she felt.

"Come right on in here," M'dear said with relief
in her voice. "I was so worried about you, I was thinking of coming after you myself."

Addy and Sarah went into M'dear's room. Addy
tried to dust off her dress and hide the hole in her
stocking, but then she remembered that M'dear
couldn't see them.

"Addy, what took you so long?" M'dear asked.

Addy and Sarah glanced at one another.

"The druggist in the neighborhood didn't have the medicine, so we had to go to another store," Addy explained. Her voice was trembling a little. She was telling the truth, at least part of it. When Addy handed M'dear the medicine, M'dear reached for Addy's hand and held it in her own. M'dear's eyes looked right into Addy's.

"There's something else," M'dear said gently. "I can tell by your voice."

Reluctantly, Addy started telling the story. When she got to the part about being forced off the streetcar, Addy said, "We was just minding our own business, and the conductor threw all of us colored people off. That ain't right."

"No, it's not right," M'dear said.

"I don't understand," Sarah piped up. "I thought colored people in the North supposed to be free. But we're in the North and we ain't free."

M'dear was quiet for a moment, and then she answered, "You're right, Sarah, we still have to fight for our freedom here in the North. That's because some people are prejudiced. Prejudice blinds people. It doesn't allow them to see people for who they really are. That conductor who mistreated you girls is blind, blinder than me."

"I don't see why Philadelphia is called the 'City of Brotherly Love,'" Addy said. "The druggist across town didn't want to wait on us because we colored. We can't ride inside the streetcars because we colored. We can't go into Natkin's Confectionery to get ice cream because we colored. My poppa can't even get a job as a carpenter because he colored. There ain't any brotherly love in this city, and it ain't ever gonna change."

"Why do you feel things won't ever change?" M'dear asked.

"Because we can't change the color of our skin," Addy answered.

"Well, you're right about that," M'dear agreed. "We *can't* change the color of our skin. But don't let prejudice make you its prisoner. Remember Sunny. His spirit goes beyond his cage with every note he sings." Gently, M'dear put her hand on Addy's cheek. "You have to keep right on living, right on singing your song."

After Sarah had gone home, Poppa stopped by the boarding house to take Addy with him on his last deliveries. As they rolled along on the slow-moving wagon, Poppa asked Addy how the day had gone with Sarah. Addy told him about their picnic and Double Dutch, but not about the trip to the druggist's and the trouble on the streetcar. Poppa had a solemn look on his face, and Addy didn't think he needed to hear any bad news.

"I looked for a job today on my meal break," Poppa said. "I heard they was hiring carpenters for a warehouse going up over near the docks. When I went there, it was the same old story. The foreman told me he didn't hire colored folks."

Addy encouraged Poppa. "Well, that man was blind. He couldn't see you for who you is, one of the best carpenters in all of Philadelphia."

Poppa put an arm around Addy's shoulders and smiled. He said, "Well, listen to you. Don't you sound like a wise old lady?"

"It's true, though, Poppa," Addy said. "Somebody gonna hire you for carpenter work, someday. I just know they will."

"I hope you right, Addy," said Poppa.

On Poppa's last stop, Addy waited in the wagon
while Poppa hauled the heavy blocks of ice inside. She
heard a bird start singing. It reminded her of Sunny,
and Addy turned to see where the bird was. She didn't
see it, but when she turned, she saw a sign posted on a
building next to the one Poppa had gone in. The sign
read, "CARPENTERS WANTED, APPLY WITHIN."
Addy jumped down from the wagon to find Poppa. He
was coming out of the building just then. Addy rushed
to him and told him about the sign.

"You should go in and see what they have to say,"
Addy said.

Poppa stood for a moment looking at Addy. "I know
what they gonna say, but I'll ask anyway."

Poppa walked up to the building and knocked
firmly on the door. Addy stood right beside him.

A white man with a beard answered the door. His
beard was filled with sawdust.

"My name is Ben Walker, and I come to see about
the carpenter job," Poppa said in a strong, sure voice.

"I'm Miles Roberts. Have you done carpentry
before?" the man asked.

"I sure have, Mr. Roberts," Poppa said. "I'll tell you

right now that I can't read or write yet, but I know how to work wood. I can do everything from build a stairway or a fence to lay a floor or frame a window. I got plenty of knowledge right up here." Poppa tapped his finger to his head. "And I got a strong pair of hands. All I'm asking for is a chance."

"Do you have your own tools?" Mr. Roberts asked.

Poppa answered, "I got a few—a hammer, a saw, and a plane."

Mr. Roberts rubbed his beard. "I'll tell you what," he said. "Come back here on Monday morning at six o'clock sharp, and I'll put you to work."

"Yes, sir," Poppa said heartily. "I'll be here."

Mr. Roberts shook Poppa's hand and shut the door. Poppa swept Addy up in his arms and spun her around.

When he put her down, Addy said, "I told you, Poppa. Someday somebody was gonna see you for who you really is!"

She and Poppa climbed back in the wagon. Poppa grinned. "Your momma is gonna be so happy," he said.

As they headed down the street atop the wagon, the sun was setting. Poppa began to whistle a song Addy had never heard before. It was a song full of hope.

Changes in
the Wind

ddy was happy when she woke up on
Sunday morning. Momma and Poppa
wouldn't have to work. It was a sunny
spring day, and Poppa would start his carpenter job
tomorrow.

After breakfast, Addy and Momma and Poppa
went to church. Reverend Drake preached about
being ready because a change was coming. He said
the war would be over any day now, and when it was,
a change would come sweeping through the country
like the gusty winds of spring. Addy hoped that what
the Reverend said might be true.

After church, Addy and her parents went back
to the boarding house to eat dinner with the other
boarders. Then they went to Washington Square Park.
Addy brought the jump rope Sarah had given her, and

Momma and Poppa turned it while she showed them how well she could jump Double Dutch.

"How in the world did you learn to jump rope so good?" Poppa asked with pride.

Addy kept jumping as she answered, "Sarah and M'dear taught me."

"I can understand Sarah teaching you, but how could M'dear?" Momma asked. "She blind."

"She's blind, but she has a way of seeing things real clear," Addy said. "She's been teaching me how to see with my ears and sing with my heart."

"Are you riddling me?" asked Poppa. "You sound just like your brother."

"No, it's not a riddle, Poppa," Addy said. "M'dear know all about the world. She been around since God invented dirt!"

As the afternoon turned to evening, Addy and Poppa and Momma headed home.

"When are you gonna pick your birthday, Addy?" Momma asked as they walked along. "Your poppa's got that ice cream freezer fixed and ready."

"I'm waiting for an almost-perfect day," answered Addy. "But I think it's coming soon."

"Well, it better hurry," said Momma. "I'm getting real hungry for ice cream."

That night Addy was awakened suddenly by a noise out in the street. She didn't know what it was at first. Poppa had already jumped up from the bed. He was looking out the window.

"What's all that fuss out there?" Momma asked sleepily.

Addy was fully awake by then. She heard three big booms that rattled the panes of the window.

"That's cannon fire," Poppa said. "It's got to be coming from the harbor."

Suddenly, there were more booms, and then popping noises that sounded like shots cracking through the air.

"Maybe the war's come to Philadelphia," said Momma with alarm.

Poppa started to answer, but the sound of people cheering, whistles blowing, and church bells ringing drowned out his words. Addy's heart started beating faster. *All this noise, and at this time of night. I bet I know what's happened!* Addy thought. She jumped out of bed and joined Poppa at the window. Down below, the street was beginning to fill with people.

"Momma, get up!" Addy urged as she turned from the window to look at Momma. "I think the war is over!" Addy started jumping up and down.

"I think Addy right, Ruth. That's got to be it," Poppa said. He went over to Momma. She was crying, and so was Poppa. Addy went to the bed and put her arms around them.

"Don't cry," Addy said. But Addy was so happy, she thought she was going to cry, too.

Poppa and Momma dried their eyes, and Momma said, "This mean we gonna get a chance to see Esther and Sam again. This the day we all been waiting for."

"Come on, let's get dressed and go on out," Poppa said. "I know I can't go back to sleep now."

They all dressed quickly. As they rushed downstairs, they met some of the other boarders, half-dressed and talking excitedly. Addy, Poppa, and Momma went outside.

Someone in the crowded street yelled, "General Lee has surrendered!"

Another cried, "The war is over! The North has won!"

Addy looked back to the house and saw M'dear at a window.

"M'dear!" Addy called over the noise of the crowd. "I wish you could see all this!"

"In my way, I can," M'dear called back.

Poppa took Addy's hand and led her and Momma into the street. As they joined the crowd of people, someone handed them lanterns and banners. Hundreds of people, young and old, black and white, filled the street and sidewalks. They were crying and hugging, laughing and cheering. Some were still in their nightclothes. They were beating pie tins and pots and pans. One man beat a drum and another played a fiddle. Firecrackers popped all around them. Addy looked up to see flags and red, white, and blue bunting draped on buildings.

This just like a dream, Addy thought. She looked up at the huge banners being held up on sticks high above the crowd. The banners waved gently in the breeze, and Addy began reading them aloud. *"LINCOLN AND LIBERTY!" "ONE PEOPLE, ONE COUNTRY."*

"AMERICA: NORTH AND SOUTH, UNITED AGAIN!"
This was the day she had been waiting for. It was not perfect. If it were, her brother and sister would be right there with her, but this was the best day she could imagine without them.

She turned to Momma and Poppa. "I want today to be my birthday," Addy said.

"You picked one fine day for it," Poppa replied. "We should go on back home and have a party. The freezer I fixed is just waiting to make ice cream."

As they made their way back home, Addy spotted some familiar faces in the crowd—Sarah and her parents. Addy rushed up to Sarah and threw her arms around her.

"I can't believe it," Sarah cried out. "The war really over."

"At last!" Addy said. "And guess what?" She didn't give Sarah a chance to answer. "I'm having my birthday right now, and a party, and you and your momma and poppa got to come!"

"Addy!" laughed Sarah. "You sure picked a good birthday. The ninth of April is a day nobody will ever forget!"

When Addy's and Sarah's families arrived at the
boarding house, every room was lit up. They went
inside to find Mr. and Mrs. Golden, M'dear, and the
boarders talking in the dining room. Poppa made his
way through the room shaking hands and hugging
everyone. Then he hopped up on a chair and made an
announcement. "Today is my daughter's tenth birthday,
and you all invited to a party right here in this dining
room. I'm gonna make a freezer full of ice cream!"

Everyone cheered and Momma said, "Addy, you
and Sarah stay out of the way till we get things set up
for the party."

"Momma, can we go out and jump rope till then?"
asked Addy.

"Yes, but stay on the sidewalk right in front of the
house," Momma said. "And Poppa, get started on that
ice cream. If you don't, we'll be having it for breakfast."

Outside, Addy and Sarah took turns jumping rope.
Addy jumped better than she ever had before. Some
people who were coming back from the celebration
joined in their game, jumping in and missing and
then trying again. Two strangers offered to turn the
ropes for the girls so that Addy and Sarah could jump

together. Other people stood by, clapping to the rhythm of their jumping.

"Listen to the ropes," Addy told them. "They singing out a rhythm."

It didn't seem long before Momma came out to tell Addy and Sarah that the ice cream was ready and the party would be starting. The girls went inside.

When Addy entered the dining room, she gasped. "Oh, Momma. It's so beautiful."

Mrs. Golden and Momma had set the tables with pretty bowls and lavender glasses. There were shiny copper pitchers of ginger pop. In the center of each table were flowers. Poppa carried in the ice cream freezer. He removed the paddle from inside and began dishing out scoops of ice cream. Mrs. Golden brought in two cherry pies from the pie safe.

"I was saving these for tomorrow's dinner," said Mrs. Golden, "but tonight is a real celebration for Addy and for all of us. We'll have them now."

Momma led Addy to one table, and there at her place was a tin of benne candies from M'dear. M'dear handed her something else wrapped in tissue paper. "You sure did pick a special day for your birthday," said M'dear. "This is from Sunny and me."

Addy opened the gift to find two of Sunny's bright yellow feathers tied together with a bow. Addy held them gently, a bit of bright sunshine in the palm of her hand.

"Thank you," Addy said. She pinned the feathers in her hair and kissed M'dear.

"Let these remind you to always let your spirit sing out," said M'dear.

"I will," promised Addy. "I will."

Seeds of Hope

CHAPTER 6

wo months after her birthday celebration, Addy stood in the middle of the garden with her eyes closed and her face tilted up to the late afternoon sun. She loved the feel of its warmth on her face.

Poppa called to Addy, "What you doing? Resting? You supposed to be breaking up the ground so we can plant some seeds."

Addy smiled at Poppa. "I'm trying," she said. "But it's hard, Poppa."

"Of course it's hard," said Momma, who was working with a pitchfork. "Nothing good come easy."

"I don't mean that kind of hard," said Addy. "I mean the ground real hard. I can't get my hoe to break through it."

"Let me help you," Poppa said.

Addy, Momma, and Poppa were working in a large garden about a mile from their boarding house. There wasn't enough room at the boarding house for a garden, so they had rented a small plot and were planting some vegetables and a few flowers. Other people had rented plots in the large garden, too.

Addy watched as Poppa easily broke through the surface of the ground with his shovel. The dirt on top was a lighter color than the dirt deeper down. Poppa picked up a big clump of earth that was as dark as coffee.

"Look how rich this earth is," Poppa said. "We gonna harvest a heap of vegetables."

Addy wiggled her bare toes in the earth Poppa had turned over. It was cool and soft. "I wish we could plant some fruit, too," she said. "I sure would like some berries."

"Well, we'll see," replied Poppa. "Remember, we ain't planting this garden for ourselves. We doing it to raise money."

"I know," Addy said. The money they would make from selling their vegetables would help them in their search for Esther and Sam. Ever since the Civil War

had ended, Addy, Poppa, and Momma had tried hard
to reunite their family. They had taken letters to aid
societies, written to the Freedmen's Bureau, and placed
an ad in *The Christian Recorder* newspaper. They had
even sent a letter to Master Stevens's plantation, where
they had been slaves, hoping someone would read it
to Auntie Lula and Uncle Solomon. But they had not
received any answers or any news about Esther or
Sam. Now Poppa was determined to go back to the
plantation as soon as he could to get Esther and to find
out where Sam might be. Poppa would need money for
his trip.

Addy followed behind Poppa, using her hoe to chop
up the big chunks of earth he turned over. Every time
she struck one of the chunks, her hands stung from the
wooden handle rubbing against her skin. Sometimes
she hit rocks hidden under the dirt, and she felt the hoe
bounce and jiggle in her hands. She dug out the rocks
and loaded them into the wheelbarrow to get them out
of the way.

Clearing out a thick patch of weeds in the middle
of the plot was the toughest work of all. The weeds
came up as high as Addy's knees. Some of them had

burrs that snagged her dress and dug into her skin. The weeds were stubborn, and Addy had to use all her strength to yank them out of the ground. Soon her back ached from bending over, and sweat ran down her face.

"Let's stop and rest a bit," Momma said. She paused a moment to wipe sweat from her brow. "We can sit down and have our picnic supper."

Momma had packed up their dinner from the boarding house and brought it to the garden. Addy was happy to think about supper—and resting. Resting wasn't allowed back on the plantation. Addy shuddered, remembering her life when she was a slave. When she worked in the tobacco fields then, the overseer watched the slaves with a whip in his hand. They couldn't stop when they were tired or have a drink of water unless the overseer said they could.

But it was different now. Momma spread an old blanket on the ground. As they ate and drank, Addy said, "If you had the chance to ask God a question, what would you ask?"

"That's easy for me," answered Momma. "I would ask what we have to do to get our family together again. I'd ask how we can get Esther, Sam, Auntie Lula, and Uncle Solomon here, safe in Philadelphia with us."

Addy turned to Poppa. "What about you, Poppa?"

"I don't know, but I might ask how I got a daughter that ask so many questions," Poppa said. He let out a loud chuckle.

Momma and Addy laughed, too. Then Addy said seriously, "I'd ask why there had to be slavery."

"There didn't *have* to be slavery," Momma said. "People chose to have it. Folks do plenty of things they know is wrong."

"If it wasn't for slavery, our whole family would be together," Addy said fiercely. "That's why I hate Master Stevens."

"You know I don't like you talking that way," Momma scolded gently.

"But I do hate him," Addy insisted. "Everything is his fault. He sold Poppa and Sam away from us. Then you and I had to run away from him and leave Esther behind with Auntie Lula and Uncle Solomon."

Poppa spoke to Addy with understanding. "What you feeling right now is a lot of bitterness," he said. "I know, because I feel the same way sometimes. It's hard not to." He sighed. Then he went on to say, "But you got to know, Addy, anger and bitterness can be like weeds. If you let them grow, pretty soon they take over and there ain't room for nothing else."

Momma poured more water into Addy's drinking gourd. "I feel angry, too, sometimes," she said. "But I feel other things even stronger. I want to hold Esther in my arms and give Sam a big hug. I want to spend evenings talking to Auntie Lula and Uncle Solomon. I want . . ." Momma stopped talking and stared off into the distance.

Addy moved closer to Momma. She knew how sad Momma was and how much she missed the rest of the family. Touching the cowrie shell on her necklace, Addy remembered what Momma had told her. This shell was a reminder to hold on to love for her family, even when she was far away from them.

"I want us all to be back together, too," Addy said softly.

Poppa stood up and held out his hand to help Momma stand up, too. "Let's clear out the rest of these weeds," he said. "Then we can start planting."

Addy worked steadily alongside Momma and Poppa for another hour, stopping only to rub dirt on her hands to keep the handle of the hoe from slipping so much. When they finished weeding, Poppa stretched long pieces of string from one end of the plot to the other to help lay out straight rows. Then he walked along one of the strings and used the hoe to make a furrow in the dirt.

When they started planting, Addy knelt between Momma and Poppa. She watched their hands carefully. Gently, they dropped seeds into the furrow and then, even more gently, they smoothed dirt over the seeds.

Addy tried to be as careful as Momma and Poppa. The seeds were precious—not just because they cost money, but because the plants that grew from these seeds would help her family be reunited. Addy knew she was planting seeds of hope.

It took a long time to plant the seeds, and Addy was tired when she finally walked to the stream to wash her sore hands in the water. But it was the good tiredness that comes from doing an important job.

"Poppa," Addy said. "Tomorrow is Saturday. I don't have school. Can I come work in the garden while you and Momma are at work?"

"Momma and I got the day off tomorrow," said

Poppa, washing the dirt from his hands. "None of us gonna go to work tomorrow—in the garden or any-place else. Don't you remember, Addy? Tomorrow the day of the big parade, the Grand Review."

"But that parade gonna have only white soldiers marching in it," said Addy. "Why we got to go see them march?"

"Because their fighting helped bring slavery to an end, that's why," Momma said. "And we should honor them for being brave."

"Well, I hope when the colored soldiers come home they have a parade for them," said Addy. "They was brave, too. If Sam ever got to be a soldier, I'm sure he was real brave."

"I got no doubt about that," Poppa said. "I ain't never known your brother to be scared of a thing. Sam is something special."

"He brave and smart and funny," said Addy. "Remember how he was always riddling me? 'Riddle me this,' he'd say. 'What's smaller than a dog, but can put a bear on the run?'"

Poppa laughed. "I got a riddle for you now," he said as he gathered up the garden tools. "What's big and red and sinking fast? The sun! We better get back to the boarding house."

"Can't I stay a little longer?" asked Addy. "I want to water the seeds I planted."

"All right," said Poppa. "But come straight home soon as you finish."

"I will," promised Addy. She filled up her watering can at the stream as Momma and Poppa left. Then she walked slowly up and down the rows, giving the newly planted seeds a generous drink of water. Addy felt pleased as she watered the garden. Her hands were still burning a little, but she didn't mind. The seeds they had planted lay safe under the blanket of rich soil, and soon, with help, they would grow.

"Well, well, well, if it isn't the little plantation girl," said a sharp voice behind Addy.

Addy whirled around to see Harriet standing at the edge of the plot, smirking at her. Harriet was a girl from her school whom she did not like.

"You look right at home in that dirt patch," Harriet went on.

"It ain't a dirt patch," Addy said. "It's a garden, a vegetable garden."

"Vegetables?" asked Harriet. "What's the matter? Don't your parents make enough money to buy food for you to eat?"

"We gonna sell the vegetables," said Addy proudly. "My poppa gonna use the money to go back to the plantation to get my sister and look for my brother."

"Oh, yes," said Harriet. "You told me about your lost brother. He's the one you think might have been a soldier." She smiled a superior smile. "My uncle served with distinction in the Third Infantry. He'll be home any day now. My mother says she expects he is a hero and will have the medals to prove it. We're going to have a big party for him."

"My brother Sam coming home, too, someday," said Addy stubbornly. "I'm sure of it."

Harriet shrugged to show that she did not care. "Well, I shouldn't keep you from your dirt patch— I mean, your *garden*," she said. And she flounced away.

Addy watched her go, feeling hurt and angry and jealous. If only she knew as much about Sam as Harriet knew about her uncle! Addy gathered her hoe and her watering can and headed home. The sun had fallen behind the buildings and the evening air was cold.

When Addy got back to the boarding house, she washed her hands carefully. Momma had set out a sheet of paper, a pen, and an inkwell on the table for Addy to write another letter about Esther and Sam. Addy knew the supplies cost precious money. She didn't want to make any mistakes when she wrote because that would be wasteful. Momma and Poppa sat next to Addy at the table and reminded her of what she should say.

"You got to remember to say where we last saw everybody," Momma said.

"That's right," said Poppa. "And make sure you tell how they can find us here in Philadelphia."

"And don't forget to say we love them all," Momma reminded Addy.

Addy smiled. "I won't leave that part out," she said as she dipped her pen in the ink and carefully began writing. Momma and Poppa watched as she wrote, their faces full of concern.

Scritch, scratch. Addy moved the pen across the paper. She knew the words she wrote were nothing more than shapes to Poppa, who could not read or write. When she finished, she read the letter to her parents.

June 9, 1865

Dear Friends,

Can you help us find our family? Please. Solomon and Lula Morgan. They caring for our dear baby Esther Walker. We last seen them last summer on the plantation belonging to Master Stevens. The plantation is some twenty miles north of Raleigh. We need information about Samuel Walker also. He about 17 years old. He was sold from the Stevens plantation last summer. We don't know where he was sold to. If you can help us, write to Ben Walker on South Street in Philadelphia, Penn. We want to find them very much because we love them all.

Ben Walker

"That's real nice, Addy," Momma said.

Poppa nodded. "You write real good," he said. "We'll take the letter to the Quaker Aid Society first thing in the morning, before the parade."

Addy held the letter in her hands for a moment. She thought about Harriet's knowing where her uncle was. Harriet could send her uncle a letter anytime she wanted to. *This letter got to get to somebody who knows something about Esther and Sam,* Addy thought. *It's just got to.* Then she folded the letter carefully. She hoped the letter, like the seeds she'd planted in the garden, would help her family be together again.

Hope and Determination

Saturday morning dawned bright and blue. Addy felt hopeful as she walked along between Momma and Poppa. They were all dressed in their Sunday best in honor of the Grand Review. Before they went to the parade, they were going to the Quaker meeting hall to deliver their letter. Outside the meeting hall, Poppa took off his hat and checked to be sure the letter was safe in his coat pocket. They went inside and walked to a small room in the back of the hall where the Quaker Aid Society had its office.

"Good morning!" a pleasant voice called to them. It was Mr. Cooper, who had helped them on other visits, his face beaming with a smile. Addy smiled back at him. She liked Mr. Cooper. He was a little man with thick, curly blond hair and a kind manner.

"It's good to see you all again," Mr. Cooper said. "How are you?"

"We just fine," answered Momma. "We hoping for some good news about our family."

"Did anybody answer our last letter?" Addy asked brightly.

"I'm afraid not," Mr. Cooper said. "But these things take time, you know."

"We been finding that out," Poppa said. "This waiting and not knowing is trying my patience."

Mr. Cooper looked sorry. "It breaks my heart knowing so many families are divided," he said. "I wish I could do more to help. Just this week, thirty people have come looking for help finding their families. I know some of them will never be reunited." Mr. Cooper shook his head. "Yesterday a young man stopped by who has been coming here for months trying to find his mother. Just the day before, I had gotten word that his mother passed away, and I had to tell him that."

Addy felt her throat tighten. She didn't want to think about her family getting news as bad as that.

She was glad to hear Poppa say in a sure voice,

"I tell you what, Mr. Cooper. My family can't give up hoping. Hope is all we got."

"Hope and determination," said Mr. Cooper. He took the letter from Poppa and smiled at Addy. "That's two good things you got working for you, Mr. Walker."

From the Quaker meeting hall it was a short walk to the parade route. Addy and her parents joined thousands of people already lining the street under banners that swooped from building to building. Addy had never seen such huge American flags or so much red, white, and blue bunting. It seemed to her that there were more people in the streets now than there had been the night the war ended. The sidewalks were so crowded that some boys had climbed to the top of light poles to get a good view of the parade.

The sounds of clashing cymbals, booming drums, and brassy horns burst through the air. Addy liked the way the music sounded, so strong and proud. Though she could hear the music, she couldn't see the musicians or the marching soldiers. She stood on tiptoe, trying to see over the people, but the crowd formed a wall taller than she was.

"I can't see nothing, Poppa," she complained.

"I can fix that," said Poppa. He lifted Addy and sat her on his shoulders. "What about now?" Poppa asked.

"I can see everything," Addy exclaimed. "This is the best seat!"

A band was just passing by. The musicians wore blue uniforms with gleaming brass buttons. Now Addy could see the soldiers, too. Hundreds and hundreds of them marched by in straight lines. Some of the soldiers rode horses. Addy smiled to see that even the horses looked special for the occasion. They pranced past with their manes braided and their thick tails well brushed. As far as Addy could see, the blue of the soldiers' uniforms filled the street. The soldiers carried rifles, and many had shining swords hanging from their belts. Addy looked at their faces. She was surprised to see how young some of the soldiers were. They looked younger than Sam.

A red-haired woman stood next to Momma and Poppa, waving a small flag. She turned to them and said, "Look! There's my son. That's Jimmy! He's the one with red hair in the front row."

"He's a fine-looking boy," Momma replied.

"You must be very proud of your son," Poppa added.

The woman wiped tears from her face as her son marched past.

"I'm so glad Jimmy made it home," she said. "My other son was killed in a battle in Virginia. Do you know what it's like to have your child die in a place you've never seen—and you never have the chance to say good-bye?"

"We can understand your feelings," Poppa said kindly. "There ain't no greater pain than losing a child."

The woman's story made Addy think of Sam. He had wanted so badly to be a soldier. Had he become one? Would he ever come marching home, proud and tall like these soldiers? As Addy watched the blue sea of troops flowing down the street, she felt tears fill her eyes. If Sam had managed to escape from slavery and become a soldier, he could be dead and they wouldn't even know it. She felt another stab of envy for Harriet. Addy tried to put the worried and jealous thoughts out of her mind, but they were like stubborn weeds that refused to be uprooted.

The next morning, Addy sat between Momma
and her friend Sarah in the women's section of Trin-
ity A.M.E. Church. Sunlight poured through the tall
arched windows, filling the church with golden beams
of light. She couldn't wait for Reverend Drake to finish
his sermon. After church, she and her parents were
going to work in the garden. Addy squirmed with
impatience.

Momma put her arm around Addy and whispered,
"Be still now, honey."

Addy stopped squirming. She settled back in the
pew, close to Sarah, and gazed at the beautiful rays of
light while Reverend Drake spoke. When he finished
his sermon, Addy thought it was time to leave. But then
Reverend Drake started to make an announcement.

"I know for many of you, the war isn't over yet,"
Reverend Drake began. "Many of you still aren't at
peace, and how can you be? The country was torn apart
by the Civil War. Just after it finally ended, President
Lincoln was killed. He gave his life trying to make the
country one again, North and South. The war has torn
your families apart. Many families are scattered, your
children lost, your fathers and sons, uncles and brothers

still not home with you. Many of you begin every day with a prayer to see your loved ones again, and end the day with the same prayer."

Addy sat up straight and listened hard. It seemed as if Reverend Drake was speaking directly to her.

"Some of you pray for healing. Maybe you have a loved one who was wounded in the war or is sick and in the hospital fighting for his life. You pray as hard as you can. God hears your prayers. He knows what hopes you have in your hearts. You know He answers prayers."

"Amen!" Addy heard several voices call out.

"That's right," Reverend Drake went on, "and you also know that God helps those who help themselves. That's why I'm asking for your help this morning."

Addy leaned forward to hear what Reverend Drake was going to say.

"Our church is going to put on a fair the second Saturday in July. We're going to work hard, all of us together, to raise money. The money will help hospitals crowded with men who were wounded in the war. It will help families who were separated find each other again. The money will help organizations that are taking care of the widows and orphans left alone by the war. Members of other churches will join us in putting on the fair so we can earn money for these important causes.

"Now I am asking each and every one of you to join in this fund-raising effort and work hard. Come to a meeting here at the church next Thursday to make plans. Will you be here?"

"Amen, Reverend!" shouted several people.

Addy squeezed Momma's hand and looked up into her face. Momma smiled back, and Addy knew that she and Momma were thinking the same thing. The fair would help families just like theirs. They would work hard to make it a success.

When Thursday night came, Addy, Momma, and Poppa were among the first to arrive at church for the meeting about the fair. The grown-ups were meeting on the first floor. When Addy went downstairs to the Sabbath school room for the children's meeting, Sarah was already there.

"Hey, Addy!" Sarah called out. "I saved you a seat."

Addy and Sarah talked while they waited for the other children to arrive. When the group from First Baptist Church came in, Addy couldn't believe her eyes. Harriet was leading the way!

"Look who's here," Sarah said.

"Oh, no," Addy said as she slumped down on her bench. "Working with her is gonna be as much fun as having a toothache." Mrs. Drake was the leader of their group. She offered all the children molasses cookies and iced tea. Addy and Sarah sat next to each other, munching on their cookies. Addy looked over at Harriet, but Harriet acted as if she didn't know her.

"Children," said Mrs. Drake, calling the meeting to order. "We are here to decide on a project you can do to raise money at the fair. Now, I think—"

Harriet interrupted in a loud voice, "I know what we should do!"

Sarah nudged Addy. "Here we go," she whispered. "Bossy Harriet!"

Mrs. Drake finished her sentence. "Now, I think it will work best if you raise your hand before you speak," she said, with a glance at Harriet.

Harriet slowly raised her hand, but a boy from

First Baptist shot his arm in the air, and Mrs. Drake called on him first.

The boy said, "We could have a pie-eating contest. Our church had one for a fall festival, and it was fun."

"But messy!" said another boy with a laugh. "Why don't we sell toy boats instead?"

Harriet raised her hand higher, and Mrs. Drake called on her. "Those ideas are not as good as mine," Harriet said. "I think we should present a magic show. I will be the magician. I can pull rabbits out of hats and make things disappear."

"I wish *she* would disappear," Sarah whispered to Addy.

Addy hid a giggle behind her hand. She thought hard while Harriet talked on about the magic show, telling the group how much they should charge for tickets, how many tickets they'd sell, and how much money they would make.

"Well, Harriet," interrupted Mrs. Drake. "Thank you! You certainly are fast at adding up figures. But does anyone else have suggestions for a project?"

Addy raised her hand and spoke. "We could make spool puppets," she said. "My poppa showed me how to make them. They real easy, and I could get free spools from the dress shop where my momma work."

"Sound good," said Sarah.

"I think so, too," said the boy who had suggested the pie-eating contest.

All the other children liked Addy's idea, too, except Harriet. "Puppets! How boring!" she said. "A magic show would be much better and much more fun."

"Spool puppets is lots of fun," said Addy. "You can make them move and dance around." Suddenly Addy had an inspiration. "I know! Maybe my poppa could even make a little stage, and we could put on a puppet show at the fair. We could tell jokes and riddles. Then everybody would see how much fun puppets is and they'd buy them."

"I think that's a splendid idea!" Mrs. Drake said. "How many of you agree?"

Everyone's hand went up—except Harriet's.

"Well, then," said Mrs. Drake, "I think we've decided. We'll make spool puppets and put on a show with them. Let's meet here a week from today to start making our puppets."

The children agreed and stood up to leave.

Addy caught Harriet's eye and smiled smugly. Harriet made a face, but Addy didn't care. Her idea had won over Harriet's.

On the way home from the meeting, Addy held Momma's hand and listened while Momma and Poppa talked about the projects the grown-ups were going to do for the fair.

"The women had a real nice meeting," said Momma. "We gonna bake pies to sell and make quilts to raffle. I said I'd bring some seedlings from the garden. All the women thought they'd sell well."

"That sound good," said Poppa. "The men gonna build all the booths for the fair. Deacon Martin got a peanut wagon, and he said he'll supply free roasted peanuts for us to sell. I said I'd make slide whistles for you kids to sell." Poppa turned to Addy. "What's your group doing, honey?" he asked. "Since we left church, you been bubbling over like a pot of hot milk. I know you got something you want to tell."

Addy smiled. "We had the best meeting. We making spool puppets." She turned to Momma. "Can you get us empty spools from the shop?"

"I sure can," answered Momma.

"Good!" said Addy. "And Poppa, could you build a puppet stage? We want to put on puppet shows so people can see how the puppets move."

"I can do that," Poppa said.

"Thank you," said Addy. "The puppets and the show were my idea. Everybody except that snotty Harriet liked my idea. She was so jealous that my idea beat hers! When she hear you're making slide whistles too, Poppa, she gonna have another fit!"

Momma and Poppa were quiet. Then Poppa said, "You disappointing me with that boastful pride, Addy. You know the fair ain't a contest."

Addy felt a warm flush of shame spread over her face.

Momma said, "I know you and Harriet hit it off like a dog and cat, but you working together now. This is your chance to make peace with each other."

"I'm sorry I said what I did," Addy replied. "I'm gonna try harder to get along with Harriet, I promise."

Momma squeezed Addy's hand. "That's all we asking," Momma said.

That night, after Addy got ready for bed, Poppa said, "Come here, Addy. Me and your momma need to talk to you about something."

Addy didn't like the tone of Poppa's voice. It sounded as if he might have some bad news to tell. He and Momma were sitting at the table. The lamp was lit, casting huge shadows in the room. Addy went over to them and asked in a worried voice, "What's wrong?"

"Nothing," Poppa said. "It's just that me and your momma changed our plans for me to go back to the plantation to get Esther. I don't have to wait until we sell our vegetables. Reverend Drake say the church gonna give me part of the money earned at the fair to help me on my trip. So I'm going in three weeks, right after the fair."

Addy threw her arms around Poppa, almost knocking him off his chair. She kissed him on the cheek. "Oh Poppa, Poppa!" she exclaimed. "It's the best news I ever heard!" She sat down on his lap.

Momma said, "You know your poppa been anxious to go. We figure now that we have the garden planted, you and I can take care of it and harvest the vegetables and sell them. We'll need money while Poppa's away and not working. And Poppa's boss say he'll hold Poppa's job for him while he's gone."

"Well, he ain't exactly promise me my job back," Poppa said. "He say if he got work when I get back, he'll take me on again. If not, I'm back where I started, looking for a carpenter job."

"Well, some bosses wouldn't even do that much," Momma said.

Addy was excited by the idea of Poppa going to get Esther, but worries began to fill her mind. Wasn't it dangerous for Poppa to go back to the plantation? When Master Stevens owned them, he could do whatever he wanted to them. Wouldn't Master Stevens be angry at Poppa because she and Momma had run away? Addy hugged Poppa closer.

"Ain't you scared to go back, Poppa?" she asked. "Ain't you scared of Master Stevens?"

"He ain't our master no more," Poppa answered, "and I ain't scared of him."

"But I'm sure he still got guns and whips, and them mean dogs, too!" Addy said, shivering.

Poppa drew back so Addy could see his face.

"Listen to me," he said. "Slavery is over, and ain't no man gonna stop me from getting my family."

Addy looked deep into Poppa's dark eyes. They looked calm and peaceful. "Is there anything I can do, Poppa?" she asked. "I'll do anything to help."

"Keep on working in the garden," Poppa said. "Don't let the weeds grow back. And something else, too." He held Addy close in his arms. "Try not to trouble your heart with worry."

"Come on now, Addy," Momma said. "You need to be getting to bed."

Addy gave Momma and Poppa good-night kisses. They stayed at the table talking quietly as Addy said her prayers quickly, dove into bed, and snuggled under her quilt. She held her doll, Ida Bean, close to her. Slowly, slowly, the gentle, peaceful sound of their voices carried her off to sleep.

Healing

uring the next three weeks, Addy, Momma, and Poppa worked harder than ever in their garden. Addy loved to walk up and down the rows with her watering can and see the little sprouts pushing up out of the earth. She pulled out weeds and kept the soil around the seedlings loose so they had plenty of room to grow.

The day before the fair, Addy and Momma gently dug out some little seedlings Momma was going to sell at the women's booth. They carefully replanted the seedlings in small pots and lined up the pots in a basket.

"I'll bring the basket over to the church," said Addy. "The children's group is meeting there again today. We made our spool puppets and now we gonna paint them."

"All right," said Momma. "But be careful with the seedlings."

"I will," promised Addy.

The basket was heavy, and Addy had to walk slowly. When she got to the church, she went downstairs to the room where the children's group was meeting. She put the basket of seedlings in a sunny corner and sat next to Sarah.

"Oh, look," said Harriet. "Been playing in the dirt again, Addy?"

Addy started to say something sharp, but she bit her lip. Addy really had meant it when she promised Momma and Poppa that she'd try to get along with Harriet. But it was a hard promise to keep. The children's group had met four times to work on the spool puppets and practice the puppet show. Every time, Harriet had been as disagreeable as she could be. Addy could see that today would be no different. She picked up a spool puppet and began to paint it.

"What that puppet going to be?" asked Sarah.

"I think this one gonna be a soldier," answered Addy. "I'll use the blue paint to make him a uniform."

"A soldier?" snorted Harriet. "That spool puppet

will look as much like a soldier as your brother does."

"Don't you talk about my brother that way, Harriet," said Addy.

"Why not?" said Harriet. Her voice was thin and high. "I bet your brother was never a soldier at all. My uncle—"

"Your uncle!" Addy cut in. "We all sick of hearing about your uncle!"

"You're just jealous," snapped Harriet.

"No, I ain't," said Addy, growing more and more angry. "*You* jealous of *me* because everyone liked my idea better than yours."

"How could I be jealous of such a stupid idea?" Harriet scoffed. "That's what these puppets are— stupid!" She threw down the puppet she had been working on, sending the spools scattering across the floor.

"Hey, don't do that!" Sarah yelled. "These puppets ain't stupid. *Yours* might be, but the rest of ours is real good."

"No, they aren't," Harriet yelled back. "We won't sell a single one! You'll see! We won't make any money and it will all be Addy's fault!"

"If you think they so stupid, then why don't you just leave?" shouted Sarah.

"That's right," said Addy. "We don't need *you*."

Just then Mrs. Drake rushed into the room. "What in heaven's name is going on in here?" she exclaimed. "Who threw this puppet on the floor?"

"Addy started it," Harriet accused.

Addy glared at her. "No, I didn't! You did," she insisted.

"It's all Harriet's fault!" said Sarah.

"Girls!" said Mrs. Drake sternly. "I don't care who started what! I'm surprised at all three of you. You know better than to behave like this, and in church, too! We're supposed to be working for a common purpose here." She looked at the girls and shook her head. "I am going to teach you girls a lesson. The fair is tomorrow. During the morning, I want the three of you to work together at the puppet stage. Just the three of you. I hope that will teach you how to get along. Do you understand me?"

"Yes, ma'am," said Addy, Sarah, and Harriet at the same time.

Harriet turned up her nose and marched back to

her seat. Addy sat down next to Sarah and picked up
her soldier puppet and paintbrush. But her hands were
shaking so from anger that she couldn't hold the brush
steady to paint.

That Harriet, she thought. *She got a way of spoiling
everything. It's gonna be terrible doing the puppet shows
with her! No one can get along with her. She just too mean.*

Addy dreaded working with Harriet so much,
she felt as if a rain cloud had cast its gloom over the
fair. She was almost surprised to see the sun shining
brightly the next morning as she and Momma and
Poppa walked to the park where the fair was taking
place. When they arrived, Addy couldn't help feeling
excited. She had never been to a fair before. She didn't
know where to look first.

There were pony rides, horseshoe games, and
booths draped with red, white, and blue bunting.
People were selling homemade preserves, doughnuts,
and popcorn balls. Soldiers from Camp William Penn
were laughing together and trying to win prizes at
the ring toss. Addy could smell fish being fried and

chicken being barbecued. Women were setting out loaves of bread and cakes decorated with light clouds of frosting. Nearby, some men were churning ice cream. Addy counted ten freezers! A group of women were slicing lemons and stirring up huge pitchers of lemonade. Addy's mouth was starting to water.

"I'm gonna find Reverend Drake and see what he need me to do," Poppa said. "Now, I know you really here to work, Addy, but take these." He handed Addy three shining pennies. "Don't forget to have a little fun."

"Oh, thank you, Poppa!" Addy said. She knotted the coins in her handkerchief. Three whole cents to spend as she pleased! How would she ever decide what to spend them on?

"Come on over here, Addy," Momma said. "I want to show you where I'm gonna be." She led Addy to a group of booths. In one, women had hung brightly colored quilts they were going to raffle. In others, they had set out pies—cherry, raisin, apple, and sweet potato—to sell.

"Oh, Mrs. Walker," exclaimed a woman at one of the booths. "I'm so sorry! I forgot to bring your seedlings over from the church."

"Momma, I'll run back and get them," offered Addy. "I know where they at."

"All right," said Momma. "You go on and get them, and be careful."

Addy hurried back to the church and ran down the stairs to the Sabbath school room. The seedlings were waiting for her in the sunny corner where she'd left them the day before. Just as she bent over to pick up the basket, she heard a funny sound. It sounded as if someone was crying, and crying hard. Addy put the basket down and looked around. The room was empty. No one was there, and yet she was sure she heard the sound of crying. Addy tiptoed over to the door of the broom closet and opened it slowly. She looked inside and gasped.

There, huddled in a corner, was Harriet. She was crying as if her heart were broken. Her face was hidden in her hands.

"Harriet!" said Addy, surprised. "What . . . what you doing here? What's the matter?"

Harriet didn't answer. She just sobbed.

Addy took a step closer. "You want me to get Mrs. Drake?" she asked. "You sick or something?"

Harriet shook her head, still sobbing.

Addy didn't know what to say. She could hardly believe this was Harriet. Harriet, who was always so haughty!

"Please, Harriet," said Addy. "Tell me what's the matter."

Without lifting her face, Harriet blurted out, "It's my uncle. He's . . . he's dead."

Addy felt as if someone had hit her in the stomach. "What?" she said, shocked. "Your uncle? The one who . . ." She couldn't finish the sentence. Her dislike of Harriet started to drain away. She understood that Harriet was a girl just like she was, whose family had suffered terribly because of the war.

"Oh, Harriet," Addy said with a sigh as she sank to her knees. She reached out her hand and gently touched Harriet's shoulder. "I'm so sorry," she said. "I truly am. I know you loved your uncle. I know you were proud of him."

Harriet lifted her eyes to meet Addy's. "He's dead," she whispered, as if she could not believe it. "I'll never see him again." She hid her face in her hands and cried bitterly.

For a while, Addy just sat there, saying nothing.
Finally, when Harriet was crying more softly, Addy
said, "I'm sorry if I was mean about him yesterday."

"It doesn't matter," said Harriet. "Nothing matters.
I know all of you hate me anyway."

"No, we don't," said Addy. "We don't hate you.
Now, you and me ain't tried very hard to get along.
We both been hateful and jealous, and I guess we ain't
never really gave each other a chance. But it ain't too
late to change. I'm sorry. I hope you believe me."

Harriet nodded. She wiped her wet face on the
sleeve of her dress. "I . . . I'm sorry, too," she said.
"I was mean to you. I don't blame you for not wanting
me around . . ."

"But we *do* want you," said Addy. "We need you.
It's just like Reverend Drake said, we got to work
together. We got to help each other. I know you feeling
bad, but will you come with me to the fair? You might
feel better."

When Harriet didn't answer, Addy went on. "Sarah
and me can do the puppet show without you if you too
shook up to come," she said. "But I sure hope you will
come." She looked Harriet in the eye and said kindly,

"Nobody else can add up money as quick as you. Will you come and take charge of the money box?"

Harriet took a deep breath. "I'll come," she said.

"Good!" said Addy. She stood up and led Harriet into the sunny room. When she bent over to pick up the heavy basket of seedlings, Harriet surprised her by lifting one side for her.

"Thanks, Harriet," Addy said. "Things sure is easier when somebody's helping you."

Harriet nodded and wiped her eyes. Addy thought she even smiled a little bit.

Addy and Harriet carried the seedlings from the church to the fair and over to Mrs. Walker's booth. Then the two girls hurried to the puppet stage.

"Y'all finally here!" exclaimed Sarah. Addy could tell by the look on her face that Sarah was surprised to see Addy and Harriet arriving together. "Come on and get to work. People already been stopping by. I already sold two puppets and three slide whistles."

"That's good!" Addy said. "Listen, Sarah. Harriet don't feel good. She gonna sell puppets and watch the money box. You and I can do the puppet show. All right?"

Sarah looked puzzled. She asked, "What's wrong with her?"

Addy gave Sarah a hard stare and said, "That's Harriet's business." Then she added softly, "Let's get started."

Addy and Sarah moved behind the stage, knelt down next to each other, and pulled a blanket over their heads.

"What's going on with Harriet?" whispered Sarah. "Why she acting so quiet?"

"She doing good just to be here," Addy said. "She just found out her uncle is dead."

"Oh, no!" said Sarah. She shook her head. "That's terrible. She must be feeling real bad."

"She sure is," said Addy.

"I never thought I'd feel sorry for Harriet, but I do," said Sarah.

"Me, too," Addy said.

Suddenly, a voice called from in front of the stage, "Where's the show?"

Addy and Sarah looked at each other. "We better start," said Addy. She took a soldier from the pile of spool puppets and Sarah took a dog. The two girls made their puppets skip across the stage.

Then Addy said in a deep voice, pretending to be the soldier, "Riddle me this. If you found a chicken egg on top of a fence post, how could you tell where it came from?"

Sarah barked like a dog and said, "I don't know."

"That's easy," Addy made the soldier say. "Chicken eggs come from chickens!"

Addy and Sarah grinned at each other when they heard the people out front laughing. They told a few more riddles and jokes. Then Addy made the puppets dance while Sarah played a song on a slide whistle. When Addy and Sarah came out from behind the stage, they were surprised to see that so many children had gathered. They smiled and bowed while the audience clapped.

Harriet waited until the clapping died down, and then she said, "You can buy the spool puppets and slide whistles here. The puppets cost ten cents each or three for a quarter. The slide whistles cost five cents each."

So many people wanted to buy puppets and whistles that all three girls had to hand them out, collect the money, and make change. By the time they'd finished

with the last customer, a new audience had gathered
and it was time for Addy and Sarah to put on another
show. It was almost two hours before they had time to
take a break.

"You were right, Addy," said Harriet. She was buy-
ing herself a slide whistle. "I can't believe how well the
puppets and whistles are selling."

"We gonna sell them all!" Sarah said confidently.
"Hey, everybody," she called out. "Come right on over
to our booth and buy our puppets and whistles. They
going fast!"

The three girls laughed together at Sarah's clown-
ing, but not for long. Quickly, another crowd gathered
and they had to go back to work.

Just before the last show of the morning, Mrs. Drake
came to the puppet stage. "Well, I see you girls are getting along well," she said happily, "and your puppet
shows are the hit of the fair. Everyone is enjoying them.
Every child I see seems to be wearing one of the slide
whistles around his neck."

"We sure have sold a lot of puppets and whistles,"
said Harriet. "I already counted the money. We've
made nearly seven dollars."

"That's wonderful," Mrs. Drake said.

"Do you want to collect the money?" Addy asked.

"Not yet," said Mrs. Drake. "I'll come back in a while."

"Don't wait too long," Sarah joked, "or the money box gonna overflow!"

As Mrs. Drake and the girls laughed, Addy noticed a tall older girl standing at the puppet stage. She was wearing a red dress. Her dress was nice, so Addy was surprised that she was carrying a big, dirty carpetbag. The girl put the bag on the ground next to the puppet stage while she picked up puppets, inspected them, and put them down.

"Hello," Addy said to the older girl. "Do you want to buy a puppet?"

"I'm just looking," said the girl sharply. "It's not against the law to look, is it?"

"No, of course it ain't," said Addy.

Just then, a large group of children arrived at the puppet stage. Addy and Sarah put on a show for the children while Harriet sold more puppets and whistles. After the children left, when Addy was selling a puppet to a soldier, she saw the older girl still lingering near the puppet stage. Then she seemed to vanish into the crowd. When Addy turned to put the soldier's money in the money box, she couldn't find the box. She looked on the ground behind the stage, beneath the box of puppets, and next to the box of slide whistles.

"What you looking for?" asked Sarah.

"The money box," Addy said in a worried voice. "Where is it?"

"Isn't it behind the stage?" asked Harriet.

"No, it ain't!" exclaimed Sarah, looking around frantically. "It's gone!"

"Oh, no!" groaned Harriet. "All our money! Somebody must have stolen it."

Suddenly, Addy knew exactly what had happened.

"It was that tall girl!" she said quickly. "The one with the bag! I just know she's the one who stole the money. Sarah, go tell Reverend Drake. Come on, Harriet! Let's catch her!"

All for One

ddy and Harriet ran as fast as they could through the crowded fair. Past the women's booths, past the pony rides, past the games they ran, nearly colliding with a group of soldiers who were pitching horseshoes. Addy's heart was beating very fast. She kept running and searching all around her for the girl with the carpetbag.

"Addy!" she heard Harriet gasp behind her. "I can't keep up with you."

Addy stopped and turned. "Let's split up," she panted. "We both got whistles. Blow yours three times if you see the girl, and I'll do the same."

Harriet nodded, and Addy ran off again. Addy thought about trying to find Mrs. Drake and ask for help, but she decided that would waste time. She had to keep running. Suddenly, up ahead of her, Addy saw a group of girls walking along. One girl wore a red dress! Addy tore over to the girls, ready to blow her whistle to call Harriet. But when Addy tapped the girl in the red dress on the arm and the girl turned around, she realized it wasn't the one who had been at the puppet stage.

"Sorry," Addy said breathlessly. "I thought you was somebody else."

She paused for a moment, unsure where to run next. She felt desperate. The older girl could be far away by now. Addy was about to take off running again when she heard a whistle blowing. One, two, three times. One, two, three times. *It's Harriet*, Addy thought. *She found the girl!*

Addy ran toward the sound of the whistle. Out of the corner of her eye, Addy saw the girl running past the women's booths, clutching the carpetbag close to her. Harriet was right behind her.

Addy joined in the chase, her arms and legs pumping hard, her heart pounding, and her whistle bouncing against her chest. Harriet was closing in fast on the girl, when suddenly, *slam!* The older girl turned and swung the bag with all her might, knocking Harriet down with a sickening thud.

Addy heard Harriet cry out in pain. Addy raced to see if she was hurt, but Harriet yelled, "Go, Addy! Don't let her get away!" Two women rushed to Harriet to help her, so Addy continued the chase.

"Stop that girl!" Addy yelled, pointing at the tall girl. "Stop her! She's a thief!"

The girl made a quick turn past the food booths. Addy took a shortcut, jumping over the row of ice cream freezers. She caught up with the girl as she came streaking past the freezers. Addy reached out, grabbed the handle of the carpetbag, and held on with all her strength. Just at that moment, Reverend Drake and two other men rushed toward Addy and the girl. The tall girl let go of the bag, sending Addy crashing to the ground. Then the girl took off, disappearing into the crowd.

Addy was still holding on to the handle of the carpetbag for all she was worth when Reverend Drake helped her stand up. "Are you all right, Addy?" he asked.

Sarah and Harriet pushed through the crowd in time to hear Addy answer, "I'm fine, Reverend." Her dress was torn at the hem and one knee was bruised, but no serious harm was done. The three girls smiled at one another.

"I'm glad that girl ain't hurt y'all," said Sarah. "And I'm glad you got the bag, Addy!"

Harriet didn't say anything, but she reached out and gave Addy a quick hug.

"Sarah told me about the theft," said Reverend Drake. "We've been following you, but you were running so fast, we couldn't catch up with you."

"I had to catch her," Addy explained, still out of breath. "I couldn't let her get away with the money, not after we worked so hard." With great relief, Addy handed the carpetbag to Reverend Drake. "I think the money box is in here," she said.

Reverend Drake opened the carpetbag. Everyone in the crowd gasped when he pulled out *three* money boxes. "Why, there must be fifty dollars in these boxes," said Reverend Drake. "If you girls hadn't stopped her, there's no telling how many boxes she could have taken."

"It was really Addy who saved the day," Harriet said, "with her quick thinking."

"And her quick running," added Sarah.

"No," Addy said. "It was all of us working together. None of us could have caught her alone."

"I'm grateful to all three of you girls," Reverend Drake said. "I guess you're probably tired out. The other children can take over the puppet stage now."

"Oh, no, thank you," said Addy. "We ain't tired. We need to be getting back to our stage so we can do one last show."

"That's right," said Harriet with a happy look at Addy. "It's easy when we help each other."

"All right then," said Reverend Drake. "I'll come with you. I've been wanting to see one of your shows all morning."

When they got back to the puppet stage, Addy and Sarah took their places behind the stage and pulled the blanket over themselves. Addy picked up the soldier puppet again, and Sarah found her dog puppet.

"Riddle me this," Addy made the soldier ask the dog. "What's smaller than you, but can put a bear on the run?"

"A cat?" Sarah had the dog puppet answer.

"No, no, no, silly," said the soldier puppet.

Suddenly someone in the audience spoke out in a

deep voice, "That's an easy riddle. Even my little sister know that one. It's a skunk."

Addy's heart stopped still. She threw off the blanket, popped up from behind the stage, and looked straight into the face of a soldier who looked just like Poppa. But it wasn't Poppa.

"Addy!" the soldier cried.

"Sam?" gasped Addy, not trusting her eyes. "Sam! It *is* you!" She ran out from behind the booth and threw her arms around him. Sarah, Harriet, and Reverend Drake watched.

"Oh, Sam! I can't hardly believe you're here!" said Addy. She pulled back to get a good look at Sam, and it was then she realized that Sam was missing an arm. Gently, Addy touched the empty sleeve that was pinned to his shoulder and then turned a sad face up to Sam.

"Don't cry," Sam said. His voice was much deeper than it had been the last time Addy had seen him. "I'm fine. I lost my arm in a battle, but I'm here. I'm telling you, I'm lucky to be here. I just got to Philadelphia yesterday. And now everything gonna be all right, Addy. Now that I found you, everything gonna be all right."

"Come on," she finally said. "Let's go find Momma and Poppa."

Addy skipped next to Sam as if she were in a happy dream.

"Riddle me this, Sam," she said. "What holds a family together so tight that nothing can pull it apart?"

"I give up," said Sam with a smile.

"It's easy," said Addy, looking up at her brother with pride. "It's love."

Pieces of
a Puzzle

ot long after Sam settled into his family's
room at the boarding house, he found a job
working in a stable for a man who ran a
cab company. Sam groomed and harnessed the horses,
mucked out stalls, and cleaned the cabs. Even though
he worked long hours six days a week, he always found
at least a few minutes to spend with Addy every day.
Now his riddles were often about horses, but she still
loved trying to guess the answers. Addy never got tired
of having Sam around again!

But summer turned into fall, and fall became winter,
and still there were empty places around the family's
dinner table, and in Addy's heart.

Poppa had gone back to the Stevenses' plantation
to find Esther, Lula, and Solomon, but they had left,
and no one knew where they'd gone. Poppa had

searched several freedmen's camps near the plantation, but after a month, he had returned to Philadelphia. Since then, Addy had helped write letters each week to aid societies and freedmen's camps to see if anyone, anywhere, knew anything about her family. But no one ever answered.

On a wet and windy afternoon in early December, the door to Mrs. Ford's shop flew open. Addy and Sarah rushed inside. The door slammed shut behind them so hard it rattled the windows.

"We sorry, Mrs. Ford," Addy and Sarah said together.

"Well, don't just stand there dripping on the floor, girls," Mrs. Ford said briskly. "Go over to the stove and dry off."

Addy's mother smiled from where she sat at the sewing machine. "Y'all late getting here from school," she said. "It's so cold, I thought you'd run all the way."

"We stopped by the Quaker meeting house to see if Mr. Cooper had any news about Esther, Auntie Lula, and Uncle Solomon," said Addy. "But he didn't."

Momma took off Addy's hat and smoothed her hair.

"Well, we just got to hope he hear something tomorrow, then," she said.

"He probably won't," said Addy with a sigh.

She peeled off her mittens and held up her hands to the warmth of the stove. Addy's dream of having her *whole* family together in freedom was taking a long time to come true.

"I know you feeling discouraged," said Momma kindly. "But we can't stop hoping. The only way you get what you want is by hoping and working hard."

"Your mother is right," Mrs. Ford said. "And she has been working hard. We both have. With the new sewing machine, we'll make twice as many dresses as we did by hand."

"And that mean me and Addy gonna have twice as many dresses to deliver!" said Sarah.

"And that means we gonna make twice as much tip money," said Addy with a smile.

The whole Walker family was saving money so Poppa could make another trip to search for Esther, Lula, and Solomon.

"There's plenty for you girls to do today," said Mrs. Ford. "In addition to the deliveries, I need you to pick up two dresses for alterations and go to the dry goods store."

"We better get started then," said Addy, putting on her mittens and hat.

But Sarah wasn't ready. She was taking off her boots. "Mrs. Ford, I don't mean to bother you, but do you got any extra paper for me to put in my boots?" she asked.

"Child, what you need is another pair of boots," Mrs. Ford said.

"Sure do, ma'am," Sarah said, pulling wads of dirty, wet paper out of her boots. "These is too small, but my folks can't afford to buy me new ones yet. I'm gonna get new soles for these. That's cheaper."

Addy saw that Sarah's stockings were wet to the ankle. There was a hole as big as a half dollar in one boot, and the sole was nearly ripped off the other. Mrs. Ford handed Sarah the newspaper. Sarah took a few minutes to fold it and stuff as much of it as she could into each boot, and then she pulled her boots back on.

"The paper should last till I get home," Sarah said, "if I don't slop through too many puddles!"

The girls gathered the packages Mrs. Ford had wrapped and headed for the door.

"Y'all take care crossing the streets," Momma reminded them.

"We will," they promised.

"And for goodness' sake, don't let the door slam!" Mrs. Ford added.

Addy smiled at Mrs. Ford and made sure she closed the door quietly as she and Sarah left the shop.

It wasn't sleeting now, but there was still a strong wind. The streets were crowded with people rushing along, trying to get out of the cold. Addy held her armful of packages close to her chest to keep them safe.

"The first address is over on Commerce Street," she said to Sarah. Addy turned right as they came to the corner, but Sarah turned left.

"Where you going?" Addy asked, catching hold of Sarah's sleeve. "Commerce Street is this way, past Washington Square."

"You right," Sarah said, smiling. "I don't know what I'm thinking." As she and Addy walked along together, Sarah went on, "Things sure done changed since last year. Back then, you would turn the wrong way, not me. You hardly knew anything about Philadelphia back then."

Addy smiled. "You the one who taught me how to find my way around," she said. "I couldn't even read the addresses on the packages."

"Now you read better than me!" Sarah said. "That's why Reverend Drake gave you the most important part to read in the celebration at church on New Year's Eve."

Addy made a face. "I'm kinda nervous about that," she admitted. "The Emancipation Proclamation is hard! It's got big words in it I don't even understand."

"I can help you practice," said Sarah cheerfully.

"I'd like that," said Addy. "Come to my house on Saturday after we make our deliveries and help me."

"Not Saturday," Sarah answered. "My momma really need me to work with her on the washing. But I can help you at school tomorrow, during lunch."

"Good!" Addy said. "I need it."

On their way to their first delivery, Addy and Sarah passed the Institute for Colored Youth. Addy stopped to pull up her knee warmers. She stared at a group of students coming out of the brick building. They were carrying stacks of books, and they were laughing and talking together.

"Miss Dunn say you can be a student at the institute when you eleven," Addy said to Sarah. "That mean you and me could be here next year and study to be teachers like Miss Dunn. Wouldn't that be good?" She straightened her back and held her head high, the way Miss Dunn did.

Sarah looked wistful. "It would be," she said. Then she nudged Addy. "But we better keep on with these deliveries. My feet getting wetter every minute."

"You right," Addy said. As they walked on, she looked back at the institute, thinking how wonderful it would be if she and Sarah were students there.

When Addy and Sarah finished their deliveries, they said good-bye and parted. Addy rushed home through the darkening streets as if she were pushed along by the wind. She was freezing! Her hat and mittens were wet, the hem of her petticoat was damp, and her feet were numbed by the cold. *Sarah's feet must be even colder than mine*, Addy thought.

She was grateful when she turned onto her street and saw the bright lights of the boarding house. She splashed through a puddle, sprinted up the steps, and landed on the doorstep out of breath.

When Addy stepped inside the door, she heard a murmur of voices coming from the dining room, though it was still too early for supper. Addy took off her hat, mittens, knee warmers, and coat and went to see what was going on.

Poppa, Sam, and Momma were gathered at a table looking at two letters. Poppa smiled broadly when he saw Addy. "Come on over here," he said to her. "I want to show you something." Poppa handed Addy one of the letters. "You know who wrote this?" he asked.

At first Addy didn't recognize the letter. It was tattered and so water-stained that some of the words had run together. Then, with a shock, Addy recognized her own handwriting. "It's one of my letters!" she said. "This is a letter Mr. Cooper sent to the freedmen's camp before you left last summer, Poppa. But how did it get *here*?"

Poppa gave Addy the other letter. "Your letter came folded inside this other one," he said. "You read so good, why don't you read it aloud so all of us can hear it at once?"

Addy's hands trembled. *Please let this letter be good news*, she prayed. She took a deep breath and began to read:

Raleigh, North Carolina
October 20, 1865

Dear Mr. Walker,

My name is Bertha Gilbert and I am a volunteer with the Quaker Aid Society. Your letter, which I am enclosing, took a long time to get here. I am writing to inform you that Solomon and Lula Morgan came to a freedman's camp where I've been working. They...

"What about Esther?" Momma interrupted nervously. "Wasn't she with them?"

"Wait, Momma. Listen," said Addy. She continued reading.

They had a baby girl with them. I still remember them because Lula took special care of the little girl, who had a bad cold. Lula sat up with her at night even though she wasn't feeling well herself. Both she and Solomon appeared thin and frail. They left as soon as the baby was better—about a week before your letter came. I tried to encourage them to stay on here longer to gather their strength. But they said they were heading to Philadelphia...

Addy stopped reading. "They must be here!" she exclaimed. "They got to be in Philadelphia by now!"

"Hold on, Addy," Sam said. "Don't count your chickens before they hatched. They might not be here yet."

"But they must have left over a month ago. They got to be here!" Addy declared.

"Now, they ain't *got* to be," Poppa said. "Uncle Solomon and Auntie Lula real old. They can't travel fast. They could've run into bad weather or had to stop at another camp on the way."

"What does the rest of the letter say?" Momma asked.

Addy scanned the final line. "It say she wish us the best of luck in finding our family, and she hope her letter helped us."

"It does help," said Poppa, "and your letter helped, too, Addy. Now we know Solomon and Lula on the way with Esther."

"Maybe they're here but ain't found us yet," said Addy. "Shouldn't we start looking for them here in Philadelphia?"

"We should," said Momma. "We can keep searching the aid societies and the churches . . ."

"And the hospitals," Sam added. "That letter said they might be sick."

"I can look while I'm out on my deliveries," Addy said excitedly, "and after, too!"

"Look, now," Momma said. "I don't want you dawdling while you making deliveries for Mrs. Ford. Like she always say, she running a business. And after you finish, I don't want you running all over the city by yourself. It's getting dark early now, and them streets is dangerous."

"Me and Addy can go together," said Sam. "We can meet up when I get off work and she's through with her deliveries for Mrs. Ford."

"And me and Momma be looking, too," said Poppa. "We been working together as a family, and that's what we gonna keep on doing."

"And together we gonna find Esther and Auntie Lula and Uncle Solomon and bring them home!" Addy said confidently.

Later that night, when Addy was snuggled into bed with her doll, Ida Bean, she looked over at the table where Poppa and Sam were playing mancala. The lantern light surrounded them with a warm glow. Momma's head was bent over her sewing. She was fitting a cuff onto the end of a small sleeve. Addy loved to watch Momma's hands sew different-shaped pieces of cloth together so that they fit together perfectly. When Momma sewed, it was as if she were working on a puzzle that always came out right. There was never a missing piece. Addy hoped her family would soon be joined together like that, whole and safe.

"Who you making the dress for?" Addy asked.

Momma looked up and smiled. "Esther," she said. "It match the one I'm making for you to wear to church for the Emancipation Celebration." Momma smoothed the red cloth with white dots over her knees. "I picked out this here fabric a while back, but I ain't dare start nothing for Esther. It didn't seem right, you know. But now I think Esther gonna be with us soon."

"Momma," said Addy, "you think Esther and Auntie Lula and Uncle Solomon is warm and safe tonight like us?"

Momma sighed. "We can hope and pray they is," she said. "You say a extra special prayer for them tonight."

"I will," Addy promised, her face lit by the light of the lantern. "And tomorrow we gonna start looking for them in Philadelphia."

A Missing Piece

ddy was so eager to tell Sarah about the letter that she ran all the way to school the next day. She knew her friend would be as happy about the news of Esther, Auntie Lula, and Uncle Solomon as she was. And so it was disappointing when Sarah was absent from school. Addy was worried, too. She hoped Sarah hadn't gotten sick from getting her feet wet the day before.

After school, Addy put Sarah's slate and reader and the day's homework assignment into her satchel so she could drop them off at Sarah's house after she finished the deliveries for Mrs. Ford. She could share her good news with Sarah then.

That afternoon, wherever Addy went with her packages, she stared at the faces of the people she passed. *Is that little girl Esther? What about that thin*

old man—is he Uncle Solomon? She remembered what
Momma had told her. She was working for Mrs. Ford
and she couldn't dawdle. But she could not help looking, hoping to see the faces she missed so much.

Sam was waiting for her at Mrs. Ford's shop when
she finished her deliveries. "I went to see Mr. Cooper
at the Quaker meeting house," he said. "He told me a
couple of hospitals to go to."

"That's good," said Addy. "And I got to stop by
Sarah's, too."

Mrs. Ford looked at Addy with a slight smile. "Tell
your noisy friend that it was entirely too quiet in the
shop today," she said. "I'm counting on her to come
clambering through here tomorrow."

"Oh, you can count on Sarah, Mrs. Ford," said
Addy. "I'm sure she'll be here tomorrow."

"I want y'all back in time for supper, now, you
hear?" Momma said. "Addy got her school lessons and
her reading for the church celebration to study tonight."

As Addy and Sam headed out into the cold, Addy
took hold of her brother's hand. Sam had such long legs
that for every stride he took, Addy had to take two. She
didn't mind. She was always happy to walk with Sam.

She had missed him so much during the months when she had no idea where he was, or even if he was alive or dead.

Sam had the sleeve of his jacket pinned up. Seeing his empty sleeve always reminded Addy of the price Sam had paid for freedom. He never complained about losing an arm in the war. Addy knew Sam was proud of having been a soldier, fighting to end slavery. He had told Addy that he would do it over again.

Addy and Sam had walked two blocks when Sam said, "Girl, why you looking so serious?"

"What we doing *is* serious," said Addy.

"That's true, but looka here," said Sam. "If we do find Esther and Auntie Lula and Uncle Solomon today, you can't meet them with that stony face you wearing."

Addy smiled. Sam always had a way of making her feel better.

"Now, that's much better," Sam said. "No matter what happen today, don't lose that smile of yours."

Addy was glad Sam was with her as they walked through the doors of City Hospital. The nurse at the front desk looked up at them. "Yes?" she asked impatiently.

"Ma'am, we looking for Lula and Solomon Morgan," Sam said firmly. "They old folks, and they got a little girl with them named Esther Walker."

The nurse quickly looked through a list of names. "Not here," she said flatly.

"Maybe they was sick and couldn't tell you their names," said Addy, "or maybe they just came in today, a few minutes ago . . ."

"Young lady," interrupted the nurse. "How do you expect me to remember a couple of old people and one baby? Hundreds of patients come through here! If their names aren't on my list, there is nothing I can do. I'm sorry."

"Ma'am, can we look back in the charity ward anyway?" Sam asked. "Me and my sister done walked nearly two miles to get here, and we just want to see for ourselves."

"You may go back," the nurse said to Sam. "But your sister must wait here. No children allowed. That's the rule."

Addy was disappointed. She sat on a bench near the door and watched Sam disappear down the hall. In a little while, a large group of people came in and crowded around the nurse at the front desk. *The nurse can't see me!* Addy thought. She eased up off the bench, slid along the wall, and slipped down the hall to the charity ward. She was only halfway there when she saw another nurse coming toward her. Quickly, before the nurse could see her, Addy ducked behind a cart filled with linens and held her breath. When the nurse passed, Addy let out a sigh of relief and hurried on.

Addy wasn't sure she wanted to go inside once she reached the charity ward. The room was dimly lit and full of shadows. She could hear pitiful moaning, loud coughing, and children crying. Slowly Addy walked forward, searching the faces in the iron beds. She felt sad and scared as she studied the grizzled old men, miserable children, and bone-thin women.

"Psst!" Addy heard someone whisper. "Get over here." It was Sam.

Addy didn't realize she had walked right past him. He was sitting next to an older man whose face was so thin, it looked like a skull with skin stretched tightly over it. She saw right away that the old man was not Uncle Solomon.

"Who is this?" the man asked in a weak voice.

"She my sister, Addy," Sam said. He turned to
Addy. "This is Mr. Polk," he explained. "He say he ain't
seen anyone like Lula and Solomon and Esther here."

"But I'll keep an eye out for them," Mr. Polk said.
"If they come here, I'll tell them you looking for them."

"Thank you," said Addy.

Mr. Polk smiled. "You remind me of my grand-
daughter Charlotte," he said to Addy. "You come back
and see me again."

"I will," Addy promised.

Mr. Polk closed his eyes. "You better get going
now," he said. "I hear the nurse coming."

"Good-bye," said Addy.

She and Sam left the hospital quickly. The cold
air felt good after the stuffiness of the hospital. They
walked together in silence for a while, both thinking
of Mr. Polk and the other patients in the dismal ward.
Addy was sorry they had not found Esther, Lula, and
Solomon, but she was glad they were not in such a
terrible place.

When they got to Sarah's street, Sam said, "I need
to get some things at the grocery on the corner. You go
on to Sarah's and I'll meet you there."

"All right," said Addy. She hurried the rest of the way to Sarah's. She knocked and knocked on the front door, but no one answered. Then Addy thought she heard voices coming from the alley, so she made her way along a narrow passage to the alley, holding her nose as she passed by the privy and stepping around piles of trash. Addy saw line after line of clothes strung across the alley. They floated like ghostly shapes in the December dusk.

"Who that coming?" a voice asked.

"It's me," said Addy. She lifted a sheet and saw Sarah standing on her toes, pinning a large shirt to a clothesline.

"Hey, Addy!" Sarah said.

"I got some good news!" Addy said. "We got a letter yesterday. Esther and Lula and Solomon may be here in Philadelphia!"

Sarah's face lit up. "That *is* good news!" she exclaimed. "Just think. Your Poppa ain't gonna have to go away again, and your whole family gonna be together soon."

"Me and Sam been looking for them today," Addy said. "I was hoping you could come with us tomorrow after you and me make our deliveries. Oh, I almost forgot. I got your slate and reader and tonight's lessons."

But when Addy handed the slate to Sarah, it slipped from Sarah's wet hands and fell to the ground, shattering into pieces.

"Oh, Sarah, I'm sorry," said Addy. She knelt down and tried to pick up the pieces of the slate. "Now you ain't gonna be able to do your lessons tonight."

Sarah sighed. "It don't matter," she said sadly. "I won't be needing that slate anymore."

"What do you mean?" asked Addy. She stood holding the shards of Sarah's slate in her hands.

Sarah did not look at Addy. She took a deep breath and then spilled out the words. "My momma need me to help with the wash. My family really need the money. We make more money when I stay home and work. I ain't coming to school no more."

Addy shook her head, too stunned to speak for a moment. Then she said, "But you can't leave school, Sarah. You can't quit! Remember yesterday? We were talking about being teachers. If you leave school, how will you ever become a teacher?"

Sarah didn't answer. She looked like she was going to cry.

Just then, Mrs. Moore came out the door, carrying a huge basket of steaming laundry.

"Oh, Mrs. Moore," said Addy. "Sarah say she got to quit school. Please say it ain't true."

Mrs. Moore put down the basket. "Come on inside, girls," she said.

She led them into a room filled with laundry from the floor to the ceiling. Addy had never seen so much laundry in her life. It was stacked in baskets, on the table, on a chair, on the bed. In the middle of the floor was an ironing board. Mrs. Moore took an iron from the top of the stove, sprinkled a shirt with some water, and began to iron it.

"Me and Sarah's poppa don't want Sarah to leave school," said Mrs. Moore. "But times is hard, and we scrambling to make ends meet. Sarah's poppa's working, I'm working, and we need Sarah to work, too. There's just no other way."

Addy burst out, "But Sarah can have the delivery job all by herself. That way she can have all the tips—hers and mine. Couldn't she stay in school then?"

"Thank you kindly for offering to help. I appreciate it," Mrs. Moore said. "But those tips won't be enough."

Addy wouldn't give up. "She just can't quit, Mrs. Moore," Addy went on. "If Sarah stays in school, then someday . . ."

"Someday?" Mrs. Moore interrupted gently. "Addy, we got to eat *today* and pay for this here room *tomorrow.* Sarah needing new boots *right now.* We can't be dreaming about someday."

Addy hung her head. There was nothing left for her to say.

"Now don't go getting yourself all upset," said Mrs. Moore. "Things gonna work out. You best be getting home. Your momma gonna be worried."

"Sam's meeting me," Addy said. "I'll be all right."

Sarah walked Addy to the front door. "I'm gonna be in church on Sunday," she said, trying hard to smile. "Maybe after, I can help you practice that Emancipation Proclamation you reading on New Year's Eve."

"Sure," Addy said. She tried to smile, too. But inside it felt as if her heart were breaking, shattered like Sarah's slate into pieces that could never be put back together.

The Last Piece

 ver the next few weeks, Addy and her family kept up their search. Whenever they could, Sam and Addy and Momma and Poppa went to different churches, aid societies, and hospitals. The family placed several ads in *The Christian Recorder* newspaper. They went to the police, too. They had not found Esther, Auntie Lula, and Uncle Solomon, but they were determined not to give up.

One afternoon a few days before Christmas, Addy stopped at City Hospital after she finished her deliveries. She was later than usual because she'd had so many packages and errands that day. Her job took longer now that she had to do it by herself. She missed Sarah's help and her company, both at school and while she was making deliveries.

Addy had been to City Hospital so many times, she didn't have to sneak into the charity ward. All the nurses knew her now. When Addy stopped at the front desk, the nurse there exclaimed, "Here you are again!"

"Yes, ma'am," said Addy.

The nurse shook her head and almost smiled. "You are the most determined child I have ever seen," she said. "Where is your brother today?"

"He had to work late," said Addy, "but my momma and poppa said I knew the way here so well, I could come by myself."

Now the nurse really did smile. "You certainly *do* know your way here. You and your brother have been here so many times that you've got nearly every nurse in the hospital looking for your sister and aunt and uncle. I know it's no use to tell you that they aren't here. Go back to the ward and see for yourself. Mr. Polk will be glad to see you."

"Thank you," said Addy, and she started to run down the hall.

"Walk," the nurse reminded her. "There are still some rules that can't be bent."

"Yes, ma'am," Addy said, slowing down.

In the ward, Addy looked at each face in every bed to see if Esther, Auntie Lula, or Uncle Solomon was there. She always stopped at Mr. Polk's bed last because he liked her to visit with him. Today Mr. Polk smiled when he saw Addy.

"Hello, Addy," he said. His voice sounded stronger. "Sit down and stay a while."

Even though Addy wanted to hurry off to a nearby church to see if there was word about Esther, Lula, and Solomon, she took a seat next to Mr. Polk's bed. "You seem better today," she said to the old man.

Mr. Polk nodded. "I am," he said. "The nurses and doctors helped me get better, and you helped me, too."

"But I didn't do nothing," Addy said.

"Yes, you did," said Mr. Polk. "Your visits give me something to look forward to, something to hope for." Mr. Polk spoke slowly. "Hope is a powerful thing, Addy. It's the greatest gift you can give to somebody, or give yourself. It can see you through the worst times."

Addy thought about her own hope of having her family all together. With each passing day, her hope had grown smaller. It was now like a tiny flame. Addy had been feeling that just a puff of wind could blow it out. But as she sat talking to Mr. Polk, she could feel her hope grow bright again.

After a while, Mr. Polk patted Addy's hand. "You hurry on home now," he said. "It's getting late."

"Good-bye, Mr. Polk," she said. "I'll come see you again."

The sky was darkening as Addy left the hospital. She'd stayed with Mr. Polk longer than she'd realized. Addy made her hands into fists inside her mittens to keep her fingers warm and walked as quickly as she could. She knew she should be getting home, but tonight she felt hopeful enough to search some more for Esther, Lula, and Solomon. First she went to the church that was near the hospital. But the church was dark inside except for a cluster of candles burning near the altar, looking like stars in a night sky.

As Addy left the church, its bells started to ring the hours. They rang six times. Addy knew Mrs. Golden was putting a hot supper on the table right now, and Momma and Poppa would be worried about her. But since she was already late, Addy decided to stop at the First Baptist Church, too. It was on her way home, and if she stopped there tonight, she and Sam would not have to visit it tomorrow. She leaned into the wind and hurried along.

The sidewalk was slippery with ice, so Addy had to slow down as she approached the church. Ahead of her in the winter twilight she saw the shadowy shape of a woman. The woman was starting to climb down the church steps. She moved slowly—as if every step were a struggle. As Addy drew closer, she saw that the woman was bent over protectively, helping a small child climb down the steps. Light from inside the church spilled out onto the steps and lit first the woman's face and then the child's face, too.

Addy froze. Her heart was pounding the way it had pounded the night she and Momma escaped to freedom. On that night, she had pressed the memory of her sister into her mind—her big, dark eyes, her round face. Addy thought maybe it was hope that made her think the face she was seeing now was Esther's.

"Esther?" Addy's voice came out in a whisper. Then she shouted and ran up the steps. "Esther?" she called out. "Auntie Lula?"

The woman stopped and turned. "Is that my Addy?" she asked. It was Auntie Lula.

"It's me, Auntie Lula," said Addy, rushing toward the old woman. "It's your Addy."

Addy threw her arms around Auntie Lula and Esther. They were both so small and thin, Addy's arms went almost all the way around them. She held on to them tightly, tears running down her face. Addy had dreamed so long, and hoped so long, and prayed so long, and searched so long that she never wanted to let go of Auntie Lula and Esther now that she held them at last.

Auntie Lula pulled back. She studied Addy's face. "My Addy," she murmured. Then she turned and bent toward Esther. "Looka here, Esther," she said. "This is your sister. Remember how me and Uncle Solomon always told you about her?"

Esther nodded. She looked at Addy with her big, bright eyes.

"What's your sister's name?" Auntie Lula asked Esther.

Esther hid her face in Auntie Lula's dress, and then looked up at Addy and said shyly, "Her name Addy!"

Addy smiled down at Esther. Her voice was trembling when she said, "Auntie Lula! We been looking for

you so long! I can't believe you're here at last! Where's
Uncle Solomon?"

"I'll explain about Solomon in good time, in good
time," said Auntie Lula. "But now it's time to get Esther
and me home."

As Addy, Auntie Lula, and Esther came up the
steps of the boarding house, the front door swung
open. Momma, Poppa, and Sam stood in the doorway,
looking worried. But as soon as they saw Auntie Lula
and Esther, the concern melted from their faces. They
rushed forward and hugged Auntie Lula so tightly,
she disappeared into their arms. Everyone was crying,
including Esther. Momma reached down to pick her
up. She kissed Esther over and over and over.

"My baby, my baby," Momma cried. "Lula, you
brung me back my precious baby. You done got so
big, Esther!"

Esther stopped crying, but she reached out her
arms for Auntie Lula.

Addy looked at her mother's face and thought
Momma was going to cry again, not out of joy but

because her own baby didn't know her.

Auntie Lula took Esther into her arms. "Looka here, Esther," she said. "This here your momma and poppa and brother and sister." But Esther turned away and hid her face in Lula's chest. "She'll come around in time," Auntie Lula said softly. "She tired."

"You must be tired, too, from your journey," Poppa said. "Come and sit by the fire in the parlor."

When they were all seated before the fire, Sam asked gently, "Auntie Lula, where's Uncle Solomon?"

Auntie Lula let out a deep sigh. "Solomon made it as far as he could," she said. "He died at the last freedmen's camp we stayed in. We buried him there."

Addy's eyes filled with tears. For a long time, no one spoke.

Then Auntie Lula went on. "Solomon and me had a time of it, you hear? We had a time. The plantation turned into nothing but a dry patch of dirt. Even before the war was over, everybody knew the North was gonna win. Seem like word of it was blowing on the wind. Slaves was running off every day from Master Stevens and 'cross the way from Master Gifford. So many was leaving, they couldn't catch them all.

Soon it wasn't but a few of us left, mostly old folks that couldn't run nowhere. When we finally got news the war was over, even Master Stevens had left because he wasn't making no money. There weren't nobody to plant tobacco.

"Solomon was sick and he knew it, but he didn't want to die on that plantation where he'd been a slave. And we was determined to get this child back to y'all. So that's when we struck out for one of them freedmen's camps. Well, we got to a camp near Virginia, and Esther got sick, so sick we couldn't move no more."

"A lady wrote to us," said Addy. "She told us you'd been at her camp."

Auntie Lula coughed and took a sip of the hot tea Momma had made for her. "Lots of kind folks helped us along the way," Auntie Lula continued. "As soon as Esther was better, we pushed on. We got to a camp pretty close to Philadelphia when Solomon just couldn't go on anymore. He'd been sick for a long time, and he just wore out."

Addy buried her face in her hands, and Auntie Lula reached out and stroked her hair.

"It's all right, child," she said. "Uncle Solomon died

a free man. He hoped for that all his life long. He got as close to Philadelphia as he could. He did what he set out to do. After he passed on, Esther and I came the rest of the way here. I ain't think I could make it another step when you saw us, Addy."

"You should rest now," Momma said. "And Esther should, too. I'll go up and get the bed ready."

Auntie Lula said, "Addy, reach into my bundle and get Esther her doll. She can't sleep without it."

When Addy pulled the doll out of Auntie Lula's bundle, she and Esther said, "Janie!" at the same time.

"Who did I tell you give you this doll?" Auntie Lula asked Esther.

"My sister," Esther said. She looked up at Addy, the firelight reflected in her brown eyes. "My sister, Addy."

Together

That night, Addy was so excited, it took her a long time to fall asleep. In the middle of the night, she woke up. The room was filled with silvery moonlight. Addy sat up to make sure what had happened wasn't a dream. She smiled when she saw Auntie Lula and Esther sleeping on her bed. Addy looked over and saw Sam on his pallet and Momma and Poppa in their bed. *Finally we all together*, Addy thought. *We all here.*

The next morning, Esther and Lula were still asleep when Addy left for school. "They worn out," whispered Momma. "Be quiet so you don't wake them."

Addy bent over the bed and gave both Esther and Lula kisses so light, they didn't even stir in their sleep.

It was the last day of school before the Christmas holiday, so school was let out early. Addy was in a hurry to get home to see Esther and Auntie Lula before she went out to make her deliveries, but she had something she wanted to do first.

She ran to Sarah's house and found Sarah inside, folding sheets and stacking them in a pile.

"Sarah!" Addy exclaimed. "We found them. Auntie Lula and Esther is home with us!"

Sarah threw her arms around Addy and both girls tumbled to the floor, falling onto a pile of sheets. "Tell me the whole story!" Sarah demanded. "And don't leave out *anything*!"

So Addy told Sarah how glad she was that she'd stayed so long at the hospital with Mr. Polk. If she had gone to the church any earlier, she would have missed Esther and Auntie Lula.

Sarah sighed. "Finally the dream of having your family back together done come true."

"Yes," Addy said. "Except for Uncle Solomon, it has."

She and Sarah sat in silence for a moment, and then Addy observed, "Sarah, you got new boots!"

"They my Christmas gift," Sarah said proudly. "My momma and poppa gave them to me early. We earned enough money."

"Look here," Addy said. "I got you a Christmas present, too." From her satchel, Addy pulled a small package wrapped in brown paper.

Sarah opened the package. It was a slate just like the one that had broken.

"Oh, Addy, I ain't never gonna need a slate again," Sarah said, and tears began to well in her eyes.

Addy put her arms around her. "Don't give up hoping, Sarah," she said, holding back her own tears. "Maybe someday you can come back to school. But even if you can't, I can help you keep up with our lessons. You done taught me so many things."

Sarah dried her eyes. "Thanks," she said, holding the slate gently. "I'd like that."

When Addy left Sarah's house, she hurried through her deliveries so she could get back to her family as soon as possible. The minute she came through the door of the boarding house, she could smell supper cooking. And what a supper it was! Momma and Mrs. Golden had made everyone's favorites—smoked ham, collard greens, rice and peas, biscuits, and sweet-potato pudding for dessert. Auntie Lula was too weak to come down to the dining room to eat, so before the family sat down, Addy brought her a tray of steaming food.

Addy knelt next to the bed while Auntie Lula ate. She noticed that Auntie Lula just picked at her food.

"Ain't you hungry?" Addy asked.

Auntie Lula put down her fork and shook her head. "I can't say that I am," she said. She patted the bed. "Come sit up here. I want to tell you something."

Addy moved the tray and sat on the bed. Auntie Lula took one of Addy's hands in hers. "When you and your Momma left the plantation, I was worried about y'all," she said. "But Solomon wasn't. He knew y'all was gonna make it to freedom."

"He helped us," Addy said. "But he didn't even get a chance to enjoy freedom himself."

"Let me tell you a story," Auntie Lula said. "Uncle Solomon celebrated his freedom back when President Lincoln signed the Emancipation Proclamation. You know them masters didn't pay that proclamation no mind because the South had broke away from the North. Oh, but when Solomon heard about it, child, he came into our cabin and strutted around so proud and happy. And then he got down on his knees and thanked the Lord."

Auntie Lula started to cough. Addy handed her a glass of water from the tray.

Auntie Lula continued, "I don't want you to be sad about Uncle Solomon dying, and I don't want you to be sad when I die."

"Don't say that!" Addy said. "You not gonna die anytime soon."

"There's a time for each of us to die," said Auntie Lula. "Uncle Solomon ain't have much time in freedom, and I won't either. Addy, we don't all make it where we want to go in life. We start our journeys and have our dreams and hopes, and sometimes other people have to carry on with them when we can't." She closed her eyes and sank back on the pillows. "I think I better rest now."

Addy kissed Auntie Lula on the forehead, turned down the lamp, and sat by her until she fell asleep.

Two days before Christmas, Auntie Lula died. Addy's heart was filled with sorrow. She loved Auntie Lula, who had been like a grandmother to her. Ever since Addy could remember, Auntie Lula had looked after Addy and her family back on the plantation. She

nursed them when they were sick. Like Uncle Solomon,
she gave them advice, comfort, and friendship. Auntie
Lula and Uncle Solomon had taken good care of Esther
when Addy and Momma had to leave her behind. And
they had used their last strength to bring Esther back
to the family. Now Auntie Lula was gone. And with
her death, Addy's dream of having her whole family
together in freedom was gone, too.

Christmas passed quietly. Addy and Esther played
with the puzzle Sam had given them as a present.
Poppa had made a beautiful sled for Addy. Esther liked
to sit on it and ring the bell. But the sadness the family
felt over the death of Auntie Lula dulled the joy of the
holidays.

On the last day of the year, their mood brightened
a bit as they prepared for the Emancipation Celebration
at church. Poppa and Sam left for church right after
supper to help set up extra seats. Addy was supposed
to go with them while Momma helped Mrs. Golden
wash the dishes. But when Momma came upstairs
with Esther, Addy was still there. She was sitting on
her bed in the darkness. She had not even bothered to
light the lamp.

"Addy, what you still doing here?" Momma asked. "You ain't even dressed yet."

"I don't want to go to the celebration at church tonight, Momma," said Addy.

"Why not?" asked Momma.

"I don't think I can stand up in front of all them folks and read those words in the Emancipation Proclamation about freedom," Addy said. Her eyes filled with tears. "Uncle Solomon's dead, Auntie Lula's dead. My dream of having our whole family together again in freedom can *never* come true now."

"Oh, Addy, Addy," said Momma with a sigh. She put her arms around Addy.

Esther came over to them. She offered her Janie doll to Addy. "Here, Addy," she said. "Don't cry."

Addy took the doll from her sister. "Oh, Momma. Look at Esther," she said. "We never got to see her first steps or hear her first words. We can't ever get back the time we missed with her."

Momma was quiet for a while. Then she said, "Remember what Uncle Solomon said, Addy. Freedom's got its cost. Sometimes a very big cost." Momma lifted the cowrie shell at the end of Addy's necklace and held it in her hand. "You remember when I give this to you? We were running away from slavery. We had nothing but each other and hope."

"I remember," said Addy.

"I told you this shell belonged to Poppa's grandma, who was torn away from her family in Africa and brought across the ocean to be a slave," Momma went on in a soft voice. "This shell was to remind you that we are linked to the people in our past forever. They live in our hearts. Their lives, and their strength and courage, are part of us even though they gone."

Addy took a shuddery breath. She thought about Auntie Lula and Uncle Solomon and her great-grandmother long ago.

Momma smiled at Addy. "Do you think you can go to the celebration?"

"Yes, Momma," said Addy. "I can."

When the church service started, Addy sat in the front pew with the other children who were going to read and recite. She was the last speaker. She sat still and tried to listen carefully as the other boys and girls gave their speeches. Finally, Reverend Drake said, "We all gathered here tonight to celebrate the anniversary of the Emancipation Proclamation. It contains some important words, words that are important to many who were held in the bonds of slavery. I want y'all to listen closely now while Addy Walker reads the Emancipation Proclamation."

Addy's knees were shaking as she walked up the steps at the front of the church. The words she was supposed to read were written on a scroll of paper that she held tightly in her hands. Addy opened the scroll and looked out at the congregation. She swallowed hard. She had never spoken in front of so many people before. Then she saw her family looking up at her, their faces full of love and pride.

There was Sam, who had lost his arm in the war to end slavery. And Esther, whose babyhood had been lost to them all. She saw Poppa, and remembered the night back in their cabin on the plantation when he had first whispered the word freedom. She saw Momma, whose hope and strength had never failed. And though they were not there, Addy thought of Uncle Solomon and Auntie Lula, too, and remembered how much the Emancipation Proclamation had meant to Uncle Solomon.

Addy started to speak, and the words came easily. Her voice was loud and clear as she read the proclamation, with its words that had changed the lives of everyone she loved.

When Addy finished at midnight, it seemed as if the whole church exploded with joy. The bells rang out, not just from her church but from churches all over the city. Everyone stood, cheering and hugging and kissing. Addy came down the steps and moved into the crowd, standing on tiptoe, trying to find her family. Suddenly, she felt a hand slip into hers. It was Esther.

Addy smiled down at her sister and asked, "Where we going, Esther?"

Esther smiled back. "Home," she said.

"That's right," said Addy. "We going home together."

INSIDE Addy's World

In 1865, the Civil War ended after four terrible years. Families separated by slavery and by war began to be reunited, just as the North and South were joining together again as one nation. But five days after the South surrendered, President Abraham Lincoln was shot. His assassination made the nation's recovery much more difficult.

The years after the Civil War are called *Reconstruction* because of the efforts to rebuild—or reconstruct—the nation. These efforts took place mostly in the South, which suffered much more damage than the North did.

After the war, Congress *amended,* or changed, the Constitution to ensure freedom and citizenship for black Americans. The Thirteenth Amendment ended slavery. The Fourteenth Amendment gave citizenship to black Americans, and the Fifteenth Amendment gave all male citizens the right to vote, regardless of race.

Congress also created the Freedmen's Bureau to help former slaves adjust to life in freedom, since most did not have homes, jobs, or educations. The bureau set up schools for former slaves, helped set up colleges for black students, and provided medical help and other services.

Even so, the lives of most black people did not improve very much after the Civil War. Southern states passed laws called Black Codes that forced African Americans to work for low wages and made it hard for them to buy land. Southern states also passed laws to *segregate,* or separate, black people from white people. These laws forced blacks to use separate areas in restaurants, hotels, and other public places or to use entirely separate buildings.

It was hard for blacks to get jobs or educations in the North, too. There was less violence against black people in the North, but there was still prejudice and segregation. Addy's parents were lucky to find decent-paying jobs.

African Americans fought for justice through their churches and organizations like the National Association for the Advancement of Colored People (NAACP), created in 1909. Some black musicians, artists, writers, doctors, and athletes broke through the barrier of prejudice. Black people also went to court to fight for equality. In 1954, the Supreme Court ruled that segregation was wrong.

The modern civil rights movement started soon after, because segregation continued even after it became illegal. To protest, black people sat in places reserved for whites and refused to move until they were arrested. People of all races protested in marches. Many went to jail, and some were killed. Dr. Martin Luther King Jr., led the effort to end segregation peacefully until he was assassinated in 1968.

The civil rights movement brought important changes to America. It is now illegal to segregate people in public places like schools and buses. It is illegal to prevent any citizen from voting. Black people's struggle for equality inspired others to fight for their rights, too. The work of the civil rights movement continues today, as people of all races continue to fight for fairness in our society.

Read more of ADDY'S stories,

available from booksellers and at *americangirl.com*

⊙ *Classics* ⊙

Addy's classic series, now in two volumes:

Volume 1:
Finding Freedom
In the midst of the Civil War,
Addy and her mother risk
everything to make a daring
escape to freedom in the North.

Volume 2:
A Heart Full of Hope
As Addy and Momma make a
new life in Philadelphia, they
find that freedom brings new
chances—and has great costs.

⊙ *Journey in Time* ⊙

Travel back in time—and spend a day with Addy!

A New Beginning

Discover what Addy's life was like during the Civil War. Outrun
a slave catcher, raise money for soldiers, and help Addy find her
family. Choose your own path through this multiple-ending story.

⊙ *Mysteries* ⊙

More thrilling adventures with Addy

Shadows on Society Hill

Addy is overjoyed when Poppa's new boss invites Addy's family
to live on his property in Philadelphia's elegant Society Hill
neighborhood. But Addy soon discovers that their new home
holds dangerous secrets—and one of them leads straight back to
the North Carolina plantation she escaped only two years before.

A Sneak Peek at

A New Beginning

My Journey with Addy

Meet Addy and take an exciting journey
into a book that lets *you* decide what happens.

After dinner, Grandpa pulls out his old coin collection. He's got a story to tell about every single coin. I think I've heard all of them about a million times.

"Look, Sweetpea!" Grandpa snaps open a small plastic case and holds up a coin that's not silver and not gold. I lean closer. This is one I haven't seen before.

"This is a bronze two-cent piece from way back in 1864," he says.

"Wow! That's a million years ago!" my little brother, Danny, shouts.

"Closer to a hundred fifty," I say, doing the math quickly in my head.

"That's right," Grandpa nods. "My father had an uncle, Charley Long, who fought in the Civil War. Uncle Charley saved this coin and passed it down to my father, who passed it down to me. Someday I'll pass it on to you." Grandpa is looking right at me. It's clear that this coin means a lot to him.

Grandpa sits back on the sofa and examines the two-cent piece. "This coin was part of your great-great-granduncle Charley's first pay after he became a soldier," Grandpa explains. "He sent his money home to his parents, and his mother kept this one coin all during the war—she carried it with her every day. It reminded her that one day the war would end, and she hoped with all her strength that her son, Charley, would come home safely."

Grandpa's story gives me goose bumps. Ever since my dad took a job out of town and my mom went back to school full-time, I hardly ever see them. There's nothing like a war keeping our family apart, but I can't help thinking that I miss my parents just as much as great-great-granduncle Charley must have missed his.

Later, when I'm in my room changing into my PJs, I hear Danny making some commotion in the hallway. I open my door to check it out.

He's dragging part of Grandpa's coin collection into his room! "Hey!" I whisper. "Give me that, or you'll be in big trouble!" I try to grab the box away from Danny, but he yanks it out of my reach. Then he drops it. Plastic sleeves and cases fall out. We both scramble to pick them up, hoping Grandpa hasn't heard us.

"I only wanted to get a closer look," Danny says. "Don't tell!"

"All right, I won't," I agree, closing Grandpa's coin box. "Now go get your jammies on."

As I take the box into my room, I step on something. It's the plastic case holding the two-cent coin from great-great-granduncle Charley. It must have landed in my room when Danny dropped everything. I pick it up, snap open the case, and examine the coin more closely. Grandpa usually polishes his coins, but this one has some dirt crusting over the date stamp. I use my thumbnail to rub the numbers *1864*. My fingers start to tingle, and I feel dizzy. I close my eyes for a second and shiver from a gust of cold air. When I open my eyes, I can't quite believe what I see.

I'm still holding the coin, but I'm not in my room anymore. Instead, I'm outside, on a pier, standing next to an enormous ship. Somehow my PJs have been replaced by a faded dress. I've also got on thin wool stockings, black lace-up boots, a scratchy shawl, and a bonnet with frayed ribbons tied under my chin. Another gust of wind sweeps over me, and I shiver again. It's cold, and whatever I'm wearing isn't nearly

warm enough. Where did these clothes come from?
Where am I?

Wherever I am, there are boats—and people—
everywhere. The ships docked along the waterfront
seem really old-fashioned—they're all made of wood
and have giant sails. Workers scurry to steady huge
crates that swing from ropes overhead as they're
unloaded from the ships.

A steady stream of people starts leaving one of the
ships. Most of the women are well dressed in long, full
skirts and fancy bonnets, and the men wear suits with
long coats and tall black hats. Some carry cloth bags,
while others give directions to crew members struggling
with large trunks. A few people from the boat walk
onto the pier carrying nothing but small bundles. Their
clothes look as thin and worn as mine. These travel-
ers are all African American, and they stand in a small
group next to a stack of crates. Some are as old as my
grandparents, and there are children in the group, too.
They all seem unsure of what to do next.

I notice a horse-drawn wagon stopping at the end
of the pier. I can't help staring. *Horses?* I look up and
down the street, realizing that I don't see any cars.

I don't see anything modern. Now I don't just wonder where I am—I wonder what year it is.

An older African American man in a suit climbs down from the front of the wagon, and several people hop off the back of the open bed. The man motions my way—is he waving at me? I duck behind the crates, not sure I want to talk to anyone. Peeking around the crates, I see a girl about my age standing next to the man from the wagon. She's wearing a blue dress and a faded shawl, but her smile is bright and friendly. The group from the ship starts to move toward the wagon. Suddenly the people from the ship and the people from the wagon are shaking hands and hugging one another as though they're long-lost friends.

I'm curious about the people on the pier and the girl by the wagon. I step out from my hiding spot and start to navigate my way through the crowd. I'm almost at the wagon when I bump into a man wearing one of those tall black hats. He glares at me as if I've just insulted him.

"Watch where you're going, colored girl!" he yells. The tone of his voice makes me jump. He's really angry with me. "You people should remember to keep your place!" he adds before rushing away.

My heart is racing. Jeepers, it was just an accident! I don't understand why he had to be so fierce. Why did he call me "colored"? Isn't that a not-very-nice word for black people? And what did he mean by "keep my place"? Don't I have just as much right to be here as anyone else?

I look around to see if anyone saw what happened, but no one stops or even seems to notice me. Through the crowd, I see the girl. She's wrapping a blanket around the shoulders of a thin woman who is sitting in the back of the wagon. When she turns, the girl catches my eye and smiles. "Hello," she shouts over the hustle and bustle around us. "Welcome to Philadelphia!"

Philadelphia? So that's where I am. Isn't it known as the City of Brotherly Love? Someone forgot to explain that to the man in the tall hat.

I approach the wagon. "My name's Addy Walker," the girl says. "Welcome to freedom!"

"Freedom?" I repeat. I'm confused.

"Yes!" Addy says, taking both my hands. "You're not a slave no more!"

But I never was a slave, I say to myself. I think of

Grandpa's coins and his Civil War stories. When the
Civil War was over, slavery was over too. Grandpa told
us that lots of people escaped that horrible life before
the war ended, though. Did great-great-granduncle
Charley's coin transport me to Philadelphia during
the Civil War?

Meet the Author

CONNIE PORTER grew up near
Buffalo, New York, where the winters
are long and hard. As girls, she and her
sisters trudged through deep snow to
borrow books from the bookmobile that came
to the neighborhood twice a week. After the
girls finished their homework at night, they
crawled into their beds and read the books
aloud to each other. Ms. Porter still
loves to read books. Today, she lives
in Pennsylvania with her daughter.